# The Professor's Dog
# & Other Stories

# The Professor's Dog
# & Other Stories

David B. Schock

Copyright © 2022 penULTIMATE, Ltd.

ISBN 978-0-9894101-6-8
Second Edition

Acknowledgements

"Children of the Forest" was first published in *Modern Age: A Quarterly Review*, Vol. 54, Nos. 1-4, Winter-Fall 2012, 195.

"Dutiful Wife" was first published as the winner of the Snowbound Writers' Contest, *The Grand Haven Tribune*, February 1, 1994.

Peggy Moceri and Amee Schmidt served as editors to make this a better book. Readers Joanie Smith, Henry Ottens, Staci Stroud, and Jonathan Eller also have my thanks for employing their considerable critical facilities. Artist Stephanie Milanowski created the portraits that are central to "Fat of the Land."

Cover design, interior design, and formatting by Amee Schmidt.

This work of fiction is dedicated to the sacred memory of
Russell Amos Kirk.

*"The communication of the dead is tongued with fire
beyond the language of the living."*

— *T. S. Eliot*

# Table of Contents

| | |
|---|---|
| Introduction | 7 |
| Snuzee Babies | 13 |
| Children of the Forest | 22 |
| Dutiful Wife | 35 |
| To Be Forgotten | 42 |
| The Old Prescott | 48 |
| Mrs. Kaiser's Radio | 60 |
| Abaddon | 97 |
| Through a Glass, Darkly | 109 |
| Fat of the Land | 118 |
| The Professor's Dog | 136 |

# Introduction

The force behind all speculative fiction is "what if?" What if the laws of nature were changed? What if there were other worlds? What if the mystical, improbable (or impossible), miraculous, and even spooky/frightening were drawn in with our daily breath? What if spirits really did manifest, and life went on beyond the grave? (I believe this with my whole heart.) Speculative fiction most often is categorized as ghost stories, science fiction, and generally weird tales. All of them embody the concept of "What if our normal were this instead of that?"

I have found great joy in reading the stories of gifted authors who posed such existential questions in fiction. My mother, to her everlasting credit, got me started very young reading the works of Edgar Alan Poe (in the 1902 Raven Edition). Most of the time, I would read Poe when I was home from school, abed with some illness. "The Telltale Heart" and a fever would combine in most unusual ways.

From Poe I grew into C.S. Lewis, J.R.R. Tolkien, Ray Bradbury, H.P. Lovecraft, M.R. James, and, most important, Russell Kirk. Kirk is perhaps most recognized for his political histories (*The Conservative Mind* was the best known). But to my assessment, he was the best living author of the ghostly tale, most often a class of tale called Gothic Romance. Just my luck: I lived in his rural Michigan neighborhood and was the editor of a small, regional weekly newspaper. I owned a small farm in

Millbrook, a little village about 12 miles distant from Russell and Annette's Piety Hill in the decayed Village of Mecosta. It was Dr. Kirk who took the time to talk with me about the nature of the ghostly tale. He and Annette welcomed me into their home and into their library down the street where Russell worked through the late reaches of the night. I determined that if there were any way I ever could follow what I thought was an important art form, especially with him as my guide, I'd do it in a heartbeat.

I had the opportunity when I was awarded a Marguerite Eyer Wilbur fellowship to underwrite the costs of an advanced degree. Russell certainly had a hand in that, for which I remain grateful and humbled. He served as my doctoral mentor and advisor as I completed a degree in creative writing and literary criticism. In reality, I was studying ghost stories. They are present across cultures and must, I argued, serve some function. Entertaining in their conveyance of disease, certainly, but there is more: they help us make sense of our world by taking a VERY wide view.

There were two parts to the degree. Or perhaps I should say I wrote two dissertations…one that analyzed ghostly tales with a view to Rudolph Otto's *Das Heilige*, or *The Idea of the Holy*. (The subtitle reads thus: *An Inquiry into the Non-rational Factor in the Idea of the Divine and its Relation to the Rational*.) My opus ranged from the study of literature to the study of the phenomenology of religions. But I knew I wanted to both have an understanding *and* to be able to tell a tale. So, the second part of my scholarship was labeled by the college as "a work of demonstrated excellence." It was a collection of a baker's dozen of original ghostly tales that centered on our mid-Michigan region.

I had the chance to work with Russell during three years as I worked on my doctorate. In truth, I worked with him longer than that—before and after the doctorate—as factotum, general dogsbody, amanuensis, driver, and assistant editor for *The University Bookman*.

I witnessed that Russell Kirk—as did Edmund Burke—attested the rising generation. He welcomed thousands of young people to his Piety Hill home for Intercollegiate Studies Institute seminars, some few as interns and assistants, and some of us also as students through International College, a one-to-one matching of faculty mentors and eager and serious students. All the faculty were members of the college's guild of tutors. Oh, it was wonderful! I have heard so many stories of doctoral students who have had nothing but misery earning their degrees. How could this have been any more different? Doctoral studies with Russell Kirk absolutely were a peak experience of my life. Russell took his obligation very seriously, but also knew how important the role of imagination and joy could be to any scholar. He routinely led his scholarly charges on expeditions canoeing down the Little Muskegon River.

Dr. Kirk was nearing the end of his story-writing career, and I was starting mine. (He said that the genius had left him, but I think it more likely there were more pressing duties dealing with history and cultural conservatism.) He served as a most knowledgeable guide. He suggested the works of Horace Walpole, Wilkie Collins, Lafcadio Hearn, Nathaniel Hawthorne, Charlotte Riddell, Robert Louis Stevenson, William Oliver Stevens, Walter de la Mare, Joseph Sheridan LeFanu, Sarah Orne Jewett, A.E. Coppard, J.M. Barrie, Algernon Blackwood, Ambrose Bierce, Henry Fitzgerald Heard, Mary E. Wilkins-Freeman, L.P Hartley, Charles Williams, Charles Dickens, Peter Haining, Cynthia Asquith, Oscar Wilde, Robert Aikman, E.T.A. Hoffman, Rudyard Kipling, Arthur Conan Doyle, Alexander Laing, Henry James, A.M. Burrage, Robert Chambers, Dashiell Hamett, H.R. Wakefield, Isak Dinesen (Baroness Karen Christenze von Blixen-Finecke), Edith Wharton, Gabrielle Long, Violet Paget, Oliver Onions, Shirley

Jackson, Montague Summers, Robertson Davies, G.N.M Tyrrell, Flannery O'Connor, Isaac Asimov, Arthur C. Clarke, Mircea Eliade, Nora Lofts, Canon Basil A. Smith, and his good friend Ray Bradbury. Glory, what a reading list!

Russell was well familiar with all of their works and had known a few of the contemporary authors himself. He found Henry Fitzgerald Heard simply mesmerizing when he lectured. And Heard's stories, almost entirely neglected in this age, were some of the best. It was Heard, for instance, who was able to clearly articulate the difference between terror and horror. Russell also thought very highly of Ray Bradbury both as a person and writer; they were correspondents. Russell wrote the introduction to Canon Smith's *The Scallion Stone*, a book I've come back to again and again.

In addition, there were Russell's own books, novels, and short story collections. I ranked him with my other very favorite, M.R. James. My late wife, Jo, and I were frequently invited to events at Piety Hill. The greatest of spectacles there was likely to occur on New Year's Eve with the ancient and honorable tradition of Snapdragon…scooping up handfuls of flaming rum-soaked raisins from a Middle Eastern mezze tray. The room was dark with blue alcohol flames leaping. Russell invariably would have to go first, darting in and grabbing a handful of fiery raisins, tossing them from one hand to the other. "Ahhhgggh…. I die! I expire!" he'd shout after tossing the lit raisins into his mouth. It was most entertaining, and sooner or later almost all attendees would consume some. No one ever died of the practice although there were some warm palms.

Very often there would be talent offerings—students performing music or declaiming poetry (often Burns) or passages from Shakespeare. The Kirk daughters would be presented and would recite from memory, exhibiting their talents inherited from both parents. Last would come a ghostly tale from Russell. It might be something he'd written, or it might be something that had been passed from mouth to ear over the generations his family had lived at the ancestral homestead.

Russell had captured those backwoods stories and fleshed them out in his first collection, *The Surly Sullen Bell* (1962). Many of those stories he had written when he was studying at St. Andrews University in Scotland. I think most of them appeared in various short-story publications. Other collections would accrue: *The Princess of All Lands* (1979), and *Watchers at the Strait Gate* (1984). There were his novels, too: *Old House of Fear* (1961), *Creature of the Twilight* (1966), and *Lord of the Hollow Dark* (1980). There is a relatively recent re-collection of his short stories, *Ancestral Shadows* (2004), alas, no longer in print. This latter edition includes some of his very best stories and is edited by his friend Vigen Guroian. One of my favorites of all is the lengthy "There's A Long, Long Trail A-Winding," for which Russell won a World Fantasy Award. This edition came out ten years after Russell had walked on; he lived from 1918 into1994.

You can intuit in Russell's writing the depth of his reading and study. Rich, rich, rich.

He was no mere imitator of other Gothic masters. And while emulation is all well and good, I found early on that I needed to *not* copy into my stories my understanding of Russell Kirk's breadth and style. In the first place, I'd never have been able to do it. In the second, no cheap imitations were needed. Russell wanted all his students to be their very own best selves. While we looked up to him, he did his best to help us develop our own voices to say what we were charged to say.

My greatest achievement in my stories of that time was to have one selected for inclusion in *Twilight Zone Magazine*. This was a part of a contest, and I was named as the best new writer of the year by that magazine. Oh, that was a prize well worth having, and I think it helped to validate our efforts. At the end of my study, my doctoral examining committee was made up of a scholar each from Princeton and Harvard, one from literature and one from religion. They welcomed me into their number. Russell had been an apt guide.

I set about writing and sending out stories. For a time I kept all my rejections on my office wall. It grew full, and I took them down when I moved. Once in a while, a story would find a home, and I'd celebrate. Sometimes one would win a competition. I judged that story writing was no way to make a living, but I kept writing anyway.

This book is part of the result. There are some ghostly tales, some that might qualify as science fiction, and some simply odd…all speculative but also a part of the tradition of humane letters.

It should come as no surprise that I agree with Russell about the role of stories. In his essay "The Moral Imagination," he writes: "What then is the end, object, or purpose of humane letters? Why, the expression of the moral imagination; or, to put this truth in a more familiar phrase, the end of great books is ethical—to teach us what it means to be genuinely human."

## Snuzee Babies

We did this to ourselves. We rationalize that no one could have foreseen this. We simply did not know how it might turn out. As such we were unwitting, but complicit.

In the middle of the last century, the 21st, perhaps no other discovery had such social impact as the advent of the Snuzee Babies. Nothing else comes close to the import of those Babies.

With the coming of Snuzee Babies there were protests, but we seemed to have got beyond the ability to take action. After a flutter of coverage and opinions, Snuzee was and would remain. It was simply…Snuzee: a profound sleep to the extent that it truly was suspended animation.

You are no doubt familiar with the formulation and the effects; this super-chlorinated molecular chain that caused all measurable biological functions to cease. There was the suspension of all metabolism: no respiration, circulation, digestion, and yet there was no autolysis, or cell death. The first experiments on lab animals showed the sudden cessation of all life with oral administration of Snuzee. Those initial experiments resulted in stacks of not-living, not-dead animals. Then the scientists discovered the antidote, the quickening agent, administered through a pinprick of what then came to be called Wake. That compound had the amazing ability to restore Snuzee suspended life. …And all without apparent deleterious effects. Researchers at first could not believe that there weren't side effects. At the worst, a reanimated dog would shiver uncontrollably if the animal's body had not been brought up to temperature before the Snuzee drug wore off. So, researchers made sure they used warming cots for the revivified.

A dog that for all intents and purposes had been dead...no breath, no heartbeat, a body that had assumed room temperature, or was at least far below a life-sustaining temperature, would—when the drug was counteracted—come back to life in a span of as little as a quarter of an hour. First would come the detection of a faint and very slow heartbeat. The rhythm would pick up in pace and intensity, and then there would be a catch in the chest and the animal would take a deep breath. Shortly thereafter, the eyes would open, a tail would wag, and a few minutes later the dog would assume its legs. At most, the animal might salivate a little more than usual in those first few hours, even drool, but researchers took it as a compensating function to rewet the mouth and nasal passages.

Scientists adjusted the doses and ran thousands of animal trials before there were attempts to experiment on humans. And those humans were in dire straits...they were either terminally ill and close to death, or they were criminals who were headed for execution. Most of us thought of such a practice as barbaric.

And, in fact, Snuzee was adapted for termination cases to eliminate judicial killings. For those applications the drug was relabeled Ndlssleep...endless sleep; copywriters think they are a clever lot.

The criminal sleepers—the Ndlssleepers—were berthed in warehouses and they required no regular attendance...no meals, no showers, no visiting hours. They consistently were studied and remained in perfect states of preservation. In some cases their raiment would disintegrate, but the bodies themselves remained seemingly incorruptible. You can imagine the resulting changes in incarceration practices. For one thing, without the spectre of inflicted deaths hanging over the heads of judges and juries, prosecutors were much more likely to seek higher—more severe—charges. What was the worst that could happen? If ever a condemned criminal were found to have been innocent, he or she was simply brought back to life, released, compensated, and left to regain a life.

That application gave rise to the others, initially the aforementioned, who were terminally ill and who hoped to sleep long enough for cures to be developed. There was even a smattering of the bored: those who simply tired of life and wanted to pass years unaware and without otherwise aging.

The risks were small; only rarely would someone who had been administered Snuzee or Ndlssleep not be able to be brought back.

You can tell where all this is heading, given the title of this "story." Was it any wonder, then, that overwhelmed mothers took to seeking Snuzee for their infant children? Have you ever tried to soothe a baby with colic? Absolutely nothing will quiet the child and there is no cure except the tincture of time.

At first doctors were surprised by the requests. The majority put aside any consideration; it was not medically necessary, a mere convenience, only. But there were a few other physicians, either those pliable with financial inducements or those who truly believed that a short respite from the demands of parenthood might better serve the wellbeing of the child than in the care of a parent—usually a mother—who was ready to snap.

Hence the Snuzee Babies. Oh, we know it started out for short-term use, a break, a little time away from ceaseless responsibility, but once we learned that there were no lasting ill effects for the babies, there came another, darker use. There were women who wanted nothing more than to create a permanent state of infantile dependence. ...Mostly women who could only have one child. They wanted to keep their babies as babies for as long as possible. As Snuzee Babies—and that's where they got their names—they were more like dolls, alive, but not living, dolls.

In certain circles—the well-heeled and affluent—Snuzee Babies became quirky status symbols.

In other circles they took the place of abortions.

The de-animated babies required nothing, could be picked up and set aside without seeming consequence.

Except there *were* consequences.

These women, as they aged, didn't seem to realize they had created a real problem, and not just morally. At some point they were too old to act as mothers, even too old to be active grandmothers. And sooner or later they faced the prospect of their own mortality.

Then what? I suppose a Snuzee Baby could have been willed to a survivor, maybe some were, but what an awful legacy. The state most often stepped in—any other immediate family members would have known and countenanced the abuse and so been unfit to take over custody. Most of these "Waked" children went into the foster system with some very odd birth certificates in relation to their biological ages.

But some few of these women made more unorthodox choices at their death. God only knows if any who chose cremation took those babies with them; there were rumors. But others—when they died—had their infants placed in their arms before they were inhumed. It took a certain kind of undertaker who would follow such a dictate. But there had to have been a first, and we know now, there were more than a few.

It's not hard to imagine that there might have been a thousand Snuzee Babies buried with their mothers over fifty years. Well, I mean it IS hard to imagine, but, even so, it transpired.

The imagining is a horror: a mouldering corpse cradling an innocent and incorruptible babe in the airless dark, day after day, month after month, year after year.

And now we know exactly how many there were: 1,051. They now are the ones who matter. The rest of us—to their singular mind—are those who both sentenced them to a living death and to having created what they are now: our overlords.

This is how it happened.

On their own, the Snuzee Babies would have lain in those graves forever. But it turned out they were not altogether on their own. Isolated, certainly, but not alone.

At the time of the Snuzee phenomenon, our government was experimenting with ultra-low frequencies—ULF. Perhaps you learned that elephants communicate over vast distances through their stamping on the earth and through their deep vocalizations. Ultra-low frequencies travel through dense media like earth and rock, perhaps even the molten core of the earth. Perhaps you know that in communication we make use of something called carrier waves, waves that carry other—sometimes many other—signals.

We didn't know it at the time, but Snuzee Babies had some manner of sentience. They were not exactly conscious, but they could sense, and they could in turn signal. These signals, originating as they did under the surface of the earth, wound up being carried by ULF waves. And they went to almost all the other Snuzee Babies. But on their own the Snuzee Babies had no language.

But the Ndlssleepers did. And there were enough of them—thousands and thousands of them—who also could pick up the ULF communications. Some of them had known, before their sleep, of the Snuzee Babies and realized not only their own predicament, but that of the innocents. And so, reaching out tendrils, they communicated among themselves and gave language and concept to the Snuzee Babies.

17

Oh, it took time. But that was what they had: years and years.

What mentors! By and large the Ndlssleepers were a disordered lot; what they taught was malignant. They were, after all, a criminal element. And many of their hearts were very troubled, even if unbeating; they taught what they knew.

Over the decades, the Snuzee Babies learned not only language but mathematics, science, government, crime, and very little compassion. Worse, they learned that they had been willingly sacrificed to the perverted desires of their mothers. There was no filial attachment even if there was ghoulish proximity. I suspect a good number of them would have been classified as mad had there been anyone there to test them.

And there were new Snuzee Babies right up until the unearthing. We know now that it took about five years to create a truly learned Snuzee Baby. Twenty-four hours a day, seven days a week, they had filtered into their awareness all the knowledge their teachers desired to transmit…to all of them at the same time and from various minds who reached out to them. There was always a queue and no quality control. The learning was as merciless as the content.

And then came the unearthing.

It began with an Ndlssleeper, Thomas Masterson. He had been convicted of a murder and was decades later found innocent. He was awakened.

As a part of reparations, he was given an allowance for each year he'd been asleep. A princely sum. With him bankrolling the effort, in the same way quiet money had put Snuzee Babies beneath the sod, so, too, it raised them. At one point he had his own resurrection team. How did he know where the Babies were interred? Thomas Masterson retained his ability to communicate with his fellow Ndlssleepers and the Snuzee Babies. They could direct him. He could do nothing at that point for the Ndlssleepers, but he could and did disinter the

Babies. What a charnel house operation! Most often the team would leave the graves open, the mothers' desiccated bodies exposed to the air and rapidly disintegrating, making no effort to hide what they'd done.

The Babies were reanimated. They were kept together by their own choice. After decades of mental-only assemblage, living physical contact was highly prized.

Masterson had those from the Western Hemisphere (because the Snuzee Baby phenomenon had gone worldwide) sequestered on a farm in upstate New York. There were other sites in Asia and Germany. No one in the outside world knew they were there...except for their caretakers, all paid handsomely for keeping the secret. Of course, the initial need was for the care of babies and toddlers. And that need stayed constant for the four years the resurrection teams worked. But then the children aged normally. The thought was that they needed schooling. Except they didn't.

That's not quite true. They understood many things, but few of them having to do with interaction with others unlike themselves. They were insular, mistrustful. Any efforts at teaching kindness or forgiveness were met with cold indifference. And they shared the same thought. The ability to read each other stayed with them. What one knew, they all knew.

As teenagers they understood the value of money and set out to make as much as possible. There had been enough pathological white-collar criminals in Ndlssleep that they had been schooled in financial markets, takeovers, arbitrage, any way to turn a buck. And they did it. Within five years they controlled the markets worldwide, not that anybody knew who or what they were.

They saw the need to control the political system, too. Chimeral as they were, they could read the deep and nativist desires of the populace and promised to deliver just what their citizens wanted to hear. There arose a generation of leaders around the globe—elected or imposed—who had one desire: control. They took it, and they've kept it.

Then and only then did we begin to understand what they were. One of the first things they did was to awaken about half of the Ndlssleepers. These were the muscle, their agents. The rest they put to death, not just sleep. It seems obvious that those who were to die knew it. And they were killed by their reanimated fellows. I suppose the Snuzees might have wanted that kept secret but maybe not, because the word got out.

Within a matter of two decades our entire financial system and governments were under either the direct or anfractuous control of the Snuzee Babies…young men and women who intended to serve as our overlords. The President of The United States is now a president for life.

If there were any of their rank who dissented, I suspect they were eliminated. Among the citizenry, there were sporadic uprisings of resistance, but all of them were put down. While the Snuzee leaders could not read our minds, they could immediately share their thoughts within their own ranks. They knew that when there was civil disobedience in one place it was likely to bloom in another. They were vigilant. And ruthless. Their military was forged with a certain callous disregard for things like laws and constitutions. Inspired by the Roman emperor Septimius Severus, they believed "Pay the soldiers; the rest do not matter." They pay them well. What law does exist here now is martial law, so summary executions are not out of the norm. We no longer have weapons with which we might fight them; all confiscated.

The only hope had been that the Snuzees would age and die. They will, but not before they have created a whole new class. They confiscated babies and drugged them. And they assigned several of their number to "sleep" with them, teaching them all they need to know.

They even improved the transmission channel; no longer is ultra-low frequency required. So, they are a self-perpetuating regime. And because they take half a decade at a time to instruct the rising generation, they are extending their own lives, at least on our scale of time. Only a few of the 1,051 have passed on and their remaining number have created hundreds more.

The future for those of us who might dissent is bleak, very bleak.

And, we did this to ourselves.

## Children of the Forest

Once upon a time there was a couple—a wife and her husband—who tended the great forest. This was the work that was given them to do by the king of that land. He told them that if they would tend the forest for a quarter of a century, he would give them a great reward, a reward beyond their imagining. And so they did that work. Every day they would leave their snug cottage in the middle of the great forest and go out to tend the trees. They would trim off limbs that were dead or damaged, clear out the overcrowded seedlings that—left untended—would choke out each other, and harvest the fruits and nuts in season. Most of these they delivered to the king's larder, but of their portion they were free to keep for their own use or sell in the marketplace in the castle town. They did everything they could to make the trees grow full and bountiful.

The wife and her husband were very happy. In addition to imagining the reward promised them by the king, they enjoyed the work, and they loved and enjoyed each other. In fact, with all the joy of their lives there was but one sadness and one sadness only: they had no children. The husband said it must have been the will of the Great God that they were not parents. The wife said she was not so sure. In fact, she said, she believed that children were coming, but not in the usual way. So, every day she tended the extra bedrooms in the snug cottage, making sure that all was in readiness.

A few years rolled by in their seasons, and the husband and the wife worked all the while. In fact, they grew to cherish their work so much that they forgot entirely about the great gift the king had promised them if they proved true to their work.

One early summer morning, the wife went out to tend the apple trees. She walked out, pruners and a small saw in her basket, into a copse in the middle of a large meadow. That meadow was itself deep within the larger wood. The trees, when she had first found them, had grown only crabbed and vile-tasting apples, but her trimming and clearing away of undergrowth had given the trees room to grow, so that now they produced small and rough but very sweet apples. She was on her way this day to see how the young crop was setting.

As the wife began to cross the meadow, she admired the apple trees basking in the morning sun and all the bees and birds active around and above them. In fact, so intent was her gaze on the trees that she was distracted from concentrating on her path, and she stumbled and tripped on a protruding rock. She twisted her ankle, fell to her side, and stunned, sat there as her ankle began to throb. She had suffered sprains before . . . cuts and bruises, too . . . and knew that even a bad sprain would discommode her only for a week or so. She could rest the ankle if only she could somehow get home.

She knew there was not much danger in her situation. It's true there were wolves in the forest, but they rarely wanted anything to do with humans. Only during the harshest points of wintertime was there any threat from them. And few people wandered the forest or strayed this far off the road, so there was little danger from robbers or vagabonds. She knew that if she didn't return to the cottage for supper, her husband would set out in search of her. And she had, as was her habit, told him where she intended to work this day. She knew, too, that he was some miles distant working with the beavers to set up a dam to empond Raven Creek.

The wife had no fear or alarum, then, when from her seated position she heard the grasses of the meadow swaying as something or someone approached. She arched her back and stretched her neck to see who might be coming toward her. Then she glimpsed, perhaps thirty paces off, a parting of the tall grasses. She couldn't see what it was parting the greenery exactly, but she could see where it traversed, and by turning her head from side to side, she could catch something just out of the corners of her eyes, something that looked black, glossy. With a sharp intake of breath, the wife thought, here was an enchantment!

She sat up even straighter as it came directly toward her. At last, the movement stopped a few feet away. The woman could not look directly on this—or *it*. When she did, there was nothing to see but a shimmering in the air. Instead, she had to partially close and avert her eyes to take in what was before her. It was most like something of a bird, perhaps even a giant bird, perhaps one too heavy to fly.

But no. With a tossing aside, a kind of cloak was removed to reveal a very small and elderly woman, a woman who had been wrapped in a cloak of feathers.

"Oh, I am glad to be found by you," said the wife. "I have turned my ankle and fallen. I'm not sure if I can stand on it just yet."

"Yes," said the woman in a croak. Her voice was large but sounded as though it were rusty from disuse. "I saw."

"Were you watching me, then?"

"I saw," croaked the old woman again. Her face was leathered, nut brown. And while her hair was white, her eyebrows were thick and black. The wife was growing uneasy beneath the unblinking beady black eyes of the crone. She sat for some moments, trying to assuage the pain in her ankle and comprehend what the old woman wanted.

At last the wife boldly asked: "You seem in no hurry to offer help, so you must want something."

"Water," came the dry reply.

The wife looked about her and found the basket she had been carrying. In addition to the small saw, the loppers, and a grafting knife, she had carried her midday meal and a stoppered jar of water. It had survived her tumble and was within reach of her outstretching arm. She handed over the container and the old woman took it, pulled the stopper and sniffed at the contents. Then she drank. And drank. And drank more. At last the jar was emptied and the old woman took it from her lips. She cackled.

"That was good. And I've left you none," said the old woman with some glee.

The wife reflected sadly that some water would have been good just then and might be even more desirable later.

"No matter," said the old woman. "You'll not be thirsty." Catching the look of dismay in the wife's eyes, the old woman softened slightly. "Ah, I see you grow concerned just what kind of mad beldam you've found. You've naught to fear from me. No, I've come to do you a service . . . Your ankle? Pah! That's a matter of healing. No, what I offer is greater than pearls and rubies." She paused, leaned forward, and then pronounced, "It's children!"

At the mention of children, the good wife felt a pang in her breast. Children! All she thought she lacked in her life.

"So, you like that idea?" asked the crone. "I thought so."

"But how?" asked the wife. She knew enough about enchantment to understand that such things did not always work out well.

"These will be children who have no one else to care for them. Without you they may even die. With you there is only a chance for them, and that is not a guarantee."

The wife was somewhat dismayed, and yet her heart longed for children she could call her own, children who would gladden the table. She remained silent.

"First it is necessary that you rest. Then I will bring the children to you, for you must choose among them. And then . . . well, then you go home." And so saying, the old woman drew her raven cloak about the wife. And the wife, after a startled intake of breath, fell into a deep and dreamless sleep. She disappeared beneath the cloak as the crone made final adjustments in covering her.

It was that cloak that accounted for the wife remaining undiscovered for several days. The woodman, her husband, followed her path several times and came to the clearing. He even found her basket and the spilled tools. But he did not trip over her slumbering form, and he could not see her. To him she was not there, although there was a spot where the air seemed to shimmer. He feared that she had been attacked and maybe even eaten, and he spent days and nights in the forest, calling her name, looking everywhere. At the worst, he feared that he might find her body or anything that might remain of it, and so he looked in bears' caves, in badgers' dens, by the foxes' burrows. He even scanned the trees to see if perchance a bird might have taken a scrap of her clothing. He feared she was dead, for he knew that she would not leave him of her own free will.

On the fourth day, the husband was out searching on the other side of the forest, and the old woman returned and withdrew the concealing cloak. The wife, who had sustained no privation or injury during her hard slumber, awakened and looked at the old woman. The old woman offered, in her outstretched hand, the same jar she had received four days earlier.

"It's full again," said the old woman. "And it will always be full. Full of the best and coldest water. This jar is now yours for all time."

The wife thanked her, drank, and drank again. The water was good. She wiped her mouth and looked up at the old woman.

"Did I sleep, then, with you here?"

"With me here and with me not here. You have slept for four days."

"Four days! But my husband! What will he think?"

"He will think that perhaps you are dead," said the old woman. "He has been searching for you everywhere, in every place he can think to look, and he has found you not. He found your basket and took it away. He was crying. He mourns for you."

"I must go to him and tell him I'm alive. Oh, my poor husband. He will think I've left him."

"He does not think so. Would you? Would you like to leave him? Now may be your chance if you want." The old woman's eyes glittered.

"No," said the wife. "He is the best and truest of men. We are well suited and take joy in one another."

"So, you would stay with your goodman, then?"

"Oh, yes. Until the darkness of death takes one of us."

"So be it."

"I must seek him out," said the wife, attempting and succeeding in standing. The pain was that of stiffness. "My ankle is healed. I can go to him now."

"Would you wait if there were children to be had?"

The wife hesitated. She looked eagerly at the crone. "If that's what's to be, yes."

The elder invited the wife to go and wash in a nearby brook, to restore herself, and to return quickly.

"I will have them here for your inspection," she said.

The wife did as she was bid and returned in a quarter hour. The old woman seemed to stand alone. But something flickered by her side, and the wife was not surprised as the old woman drew aside a smaller raven cloak to reveal three very young children . . . well, children of a sort. They were part elvish with pointed ears and very delicate features.

"Are these your children?" asked the crone. "You must choose."

"If this is the only choice, then they are my children," said the wife. "But they are not like us at all. They are of the elves, and as lovely as they are, I fear they would die away from their own kind. And if they lived, I fear they would find our home too much of men and women and not enough of the wood."

"This is not your only choice," said the elder. "And you have chosen wisely so far. You have two more choices." She wrapped the cloak about the children, and they slumbered.

She turned to another spot where the grasses were glimmering and withdrew a second cloak. Here were three more children, clothed in purple, whose eyes opened on the wife with disdain.

"You, there," said the eldest of the three. "Fetch our robes and water . . . no, bring wine. What is this rude place? Who are you?"

"Are these your children?" asked the old woman.

The wife shuddered. "If you say they are. But I fear they are born to a royal estate and would find our home rustic, crude, and not to their liking. My husband and I would not be to their liking either, I fear."

"So, that would mean," said the old woman as she wrapped and napped the three royal children, "that those who still remain cloaked and unknown to you are yours?"

"As you say," said the wife as she looked upon the last trio the old woman revealed. They were human and not elvish, ragged, and not clothed in splendor. They cowered before her, hugging their shoulders.

The youngest looked up at her with golden eyes and said one word: "Please?"

The wife let out her breath and nodded. Then she knelt and opened her arms. The children, with some care, looking at each other (and all through golden eyes), moved into the woman's arms. They closed their eyes as the goodwife encircled them.

"They are yours?" asked the old woman.

"Yes," said the wife. "They are ours."

She rose and led them from the clearing, into the forest, and to the home they would share.

The old woman took the three smaller cloaks, joined them with the one that had concealed the wife, and shook them into a single garment that she wrapped about her shoulders. And, of course, she vanished.

The other children? They too vanished into thin air. They had been mere illusions, their images borrowed from the elves of the deep woods and the royals in the castle. The real children from whom these likenesses were drawn had not been so much disturbed as to have been troubled by a bad or unsettling dream.

The real children, though, had suffered from long privation. They were next to naked, hungry, and cold. The wife gathered food for them to eat as they went along, and she shared her own clothing to warm them. She also held their hands and told them of the lives they might lead.

At last they came to the cottage. The woodman heard his wife's trilling laughter and heard her shout to announce their arrival. He rushed from the front door to embrace her.

"I thought you dead!" he said, crying with tears of relief. He embraced her and was loath to let her go. At last he opened his eyes and saw the three young children around them. He started.

"Wh-wh-who are these?" he begged.

"They are ours," said the wife. "Let me but bring them inside to feed and warm them, and I will tell you all that has happened."

With great tenderness and love, the wife cared for the children as she promised. Food first, warmth while eating, then washing, and clothes of odd sizes and fit. Finally, the children were transported to slumber in the soft beds so long kept ready.

"Husband," she said when at last they were seated at the table, "these children are a gift, given to us by an old woman, an enchantress."

She went on to tell him all that had transpired . . . from her injury, the appearance of the crone, and the raven cloak to the children she was shown and from whose number she was bid to pick.

"The first were elven and would not have survived here; they needed to be with their own kind.

"The second were human children but of high estate. Never would they have gone with us willingly to hew and trim. Nor would they have borne with the daily tasks of our living. They were not for us here.

"But these who remained had need and nowhere else to go. They might become like us. They might learn to love the wood and all its mysteries. They might become our children even if they were not born our children."

The husband listened and thought. He trusted his wife and understood that her understanding exceeded his own. If she thought it so, so would he.

And so, day by day, the children increased in health, in appetite, and in a loosening of the wariness of the memories of all that had so straitened them. They learned to play together in the safety of the hearth and yard, their shouts of delight ringing through the house. They also learned to work and worked to learn. Their minds were quick, and their understanding often intuitive. They displayed no hesitancy to draw near to the fire that makes up a family.

But the husband took note of one or two oddities. How could he not? He studied them whenever he was in their presence, and he thought on them when he was absent. He noted the pattern of their walking, how their toes came down first and their heels followed. And he noted also how they moved with steely concentration when they passed through the wood, their eyes reaching out far in front of them. And how they tussled much like puppies do in their over-and-under play, full of yips and yaps. The husband decided they were human . . . but something other, too. And that other?

"Wife," said the woodman one afternoon as they sat alone together. "Our children— love them as I do—are not altogether like us or like other humans."

The wife listened attentively and looked down to study the floor.

"I have seen the animal they most resemble," said the husband. "And that is the wolf."

It was true.

The wife had noted that when she looked straight on at their faces, she saw children, happy, healthy children, but when she saw them out of the corners of her eyes, she saw something slightly other . . . a shifting of shape, a suggestion of a muzzle and brilliantly golden eyes set in the midst of grey and black fur.

"Are they bewitched?" she wondered aloud.

Her husband shrugged his shoulders. "For my part I don't much care as long as they don't eat us." And he laughed, but not entirely. And so the matter stood for almost a full year. The children grew joyously. All were of help in the household and in the woods. And they *knew* the woods better than any other human children the goodman and his goodwife had encountered.

One day it fell to the woodman to be alone in the oldest part of the forest. He had worked all morning and was just sitting down to eat his meal when he espied something shimmering before the largest tree in the wood. With a flick of her wrist, the crone stood before him, holding her raven cloak in her hands.

"So, now you've come for me," said the husband, knowingly. "How many days will I be missing? How much grief will I cause my wife and how much fear for our children?"

"No days," said the old woman. "Hours only. And those we will spend in converse."

The woodman bid the old woman seated and offered her of his provender. She ate and drank, draining his water jug as she had his wife's. He smiled at the thought that hers now always refilled itself.

"You fear your own children," said the woman. "You fear they will devour you. You fear that they are not like you, that they are wolfish. They are, but through enchantment stronger than my own. It was that same enchantment that drove their parents mad and running off on all fours through the forest many years ago. They have long since died. The children have been waiting through time, through decades and ages, to be loved as you and your wife love them. But still you are uneasy. What is to be done?"

"Can't you change the spell that's upon them?" asked the woodman.

"Alas," she responded. "I have great powers, but that is beyond even me." She was downcast.

"If there were a way," reasoned the woodman, "that you could take away my fear— for I know it's there— then I could love them as completely as my wife already does. And she might love them even better. Could you do that?"

"Perhaps, but it might engender a great change . . . in you. And perhaps even in your wife. What then? Would you still be willing?"

The husband thought a long while before he spoke.

"As long as it meant not loving my wife less—or her me—I would venture it."

"So be it," said the crone, and she threw her raven cloak over his head.

He didn't go to sleep or even grow tired. But things changed within him. He could smell the individual birds from whose feathers the cloak was made. He could scent the old woman and hear her heartbeat. And, in fact, he could see better in the dark under the cloak than ever he could outside at night when there was no moon. When she withdrew the cloak, he was himself, but different.

The old woman bade him farewell, assuring him that if ever he needed her, he had but to seek her as he had done, even unknowing.

He was mystified at that pronouncement—had he sought her?—but accepted it as a promise of value.

When he concluded his day's work, he found his way home. He was later than he had planned, but the gathering darkness posed no problems to his eyes. And the smell of the wood caused him to linger. He found himself with his nose lifted to the wind, his eyes closed in pleasure.

When he arrived home, everything was the same, but different. The children were more familiar to him. And his wife? She was as familiar as always. But she was different, too, and it came to him in just what ways after dinner as he sat sharpening his axe. When she spoke to him, he turned to look at her, but when he turned back to his axe, he saw her from the corner of his eye. Her face, her lovely face, so familiar to him, was transformed. He could detect the suggestion of a muzzle, golden eyes, and very fine, dark fur around them. He barked a laugh and understood.

"Wife, wife," he said. "It was true, they were wolfish. They *are* wolfish. But now . . .," and he laughed. "So are we!"

And he told her of his encounter with the crone. "This was her way of making us a true family."

"But will ever we be able to go among men again?" asked the wife with some trepidation.

"That we'll have to see," answered the husband. "But I have often sensed that others have the influence of the beasts upon them: the porcine, the bovine, the feline, the equine, the vulpine, the canine, even the ursine. It may be that influenced as they are, they will not notice the lupine in us."

The wife reflected on the piggish face of the butcher in the castle town. His name also fit the image: Swinehart. And there were others who embodied the animals in their visage or stance, or movements: those who showed the cow, the cat, the horse, the fox, the dog, or the bear. She smiled and thought that being in some measure of the wolf might be very good. And, besides, the smells in this world were far more interesting.

And so they lived for many years. The children grew and found mates of their own and stayed close to their parents. All lived in harmony.

If anything, those in the castle town gave them even more respect than before . . . and a little distance; for within each of them remained the slightest trace of wolf, something about the eyes and the nose. ...And their intensity.

And the king? At the conclusion of their years of service, he had them brought to him and gave them many treasures and privileges. He also gave them their area of the forest to have for all time through all generations. And those generations in turn gave service to the king and the following kings and queens to serve as guardians of the forest.

The forest prospered, the kingdom prospered, and the family of the woodman and his wife prospered.

## Dutiful Wife

Guilt made manifest.

That was it, he supposed. And everything else came from that deep sense of self-blame.

Or so he thought at the beginning.

He knew from his ministry, for example, that guilt often prodded any number of aberrations. Certainly, it could fuel a recurring dream. The living blame themselves for drawing breath, for every wrong they have ever done to—or thought of—the new-dead. This, he saw, was part of the business of coming to terms with loss.

And he had suffered loss. His wife had died six months before and her presence in his dreams was to be expected, even under usual circumstances. But there was additional reason for guilt. He saw that he was actually pleased in a way—he had to be honest with himself—that she was gone. He was relieved. Of pressures. Of responsibilities. His wife's death put an end to almost everything that had held him back in his ministry. He was now free, he supposed for the first time in his adult life, to invest all of himself in his calling, even though he no longer held a pulpit. That recognition led to an extra nagging guilt.

And sorrow—real sorrow—at her loss and the resulting disruption in his life.

As always, when he thought about her, he started with her death. The tableau ... he could see her again as she drew her last breath.

She stood lecturing him then, her face impassive. She always used Scripture to drive home her point. And since his retirement from active clerical duty, she had found all the more occasion to address him.

This time his sin was sloth. He had been caught again lingering over the newspaper crossword. Second Thessalonians: "... if any would not work, neither should he eat." There was work to do in the house, he knew, but he was, after all, old and retired.

And his heart had been paining him. Angina. But to protest, he learned long ago, served no purpose. He prepared to rise, when she sucked in air to begin speaking to him again.

"By the labor of your brow...."

She paused, mid-admonition, looked at him with great surprise, and fell to the floor.

He kept reminding himself that he did make attempts to revive her. The medical examiner later conjectured that she was dead before she hit the braided rug, the result of a massive heart attack. Insofar as he knew, she was never before sick a day in her life.

It was hard to square, this process of losing someone with whom he'd shared his life.

For more than forty-five years he'd listened to her severest pronouncements. He could almost catalogue—before the fact—from which text she would take her ammunition. Proverbs was her favorite. For all of that, she avoided lyrical passages that made mention of a wife as a delight. Ecclesiastes was fine, until she got to the part about enjoying anything during all of life's foolish days.

She was also very strong against vanity. Odd, he thought, considering her incongruous application of bright lipstick. It was, she said, her one consent to fashion. It appeared more like her one affectation ... in addition to her Bible reasoning. She carried that lipstick to her grave, carefully layered by the mortician to conform to a recent picture she'd had taken and presented to her husband on his most recent birthday.

He reflected on that lipstick and its application. In age her lips had shrunk, but the line of her lipstick had become overly generous and arbitrary. It seemed that her lips grew each year, and not always in symmetry.

Her lips had indeed once been very fair to ponder and to kiss, although opportunities had never been plentiful. He had thought her, at first, absolute perfection. She was a beautiful girl. And pious. He was a new seminary graduate, and her Bible verses had stirred admiration and reverence in him. Her purity, and her understanding of the Scriptures, were, he was sure, a sign of her spirituality. And his marriage to her was, he believed, a match made in heaven.

He was amazed, in those first few blissful months, that she was unyielding. She had never, as he assumed she would, unbent from her rigid ways. After the first year he understood his marriage. For all her pride in his position, she clearly saw her duty as Duty with a capital "D." As a clergy wife, she went through all the motions, but never was there any joy in serving God's word. She never smiled, other than a politic grimace, or made attempts to put others at ease. She denied herself even the smallest pleasures, and she fully intended that he should deny himself, too.

At first, he rebelled and tried to change her. He made light of almost everything. She not only harped about his vanity, but his silliness: "Foolishness of man perverteth his way."

He, too, loved the Bible, but as a living book, not a dead law. Every time he waxed enthusiastic—about anything, she would chill his spirit.

Not many others could come to terms with his wife either. In one parish after another he would suffer along until he was reassigned. Always there was the tacit understanding that his work was fine, but there was something lacking. Nothing definite. No, they couldn't be that harsh.

In his later years he managed to very nearly keep her altogether out of his work. He learned to live for his ministry, and she didn't seem to mind—as long as she couldn't see him enjoying what he was doing.

Divorce was out of the question. She was, after all, the wife of his youth. If it was his lot to have a millstone of his own choosing around his neck, he could not complain. He never once betrayed her by so much as seeking sympathy elsewhere.

He fully expected that only in death would he find release from his life of long devotion and very true love, both to his God and to her. For he had grown to love her, despite the pity he felt for her. Infrequently, he pitied himself. At those odd moments death looked like an old friend.

In one sense, he had longed for death. His earthly duties were done. He believed the transition from this life to the next was a doorway; more and more often he felt ready to walk through that portal. Age, too, had made him more ready to die. He was waiting his appointed time; before her death, she seemed to wait expectantly for his time, too. The actuarial tables predicted as much. And his angina had been steadily worsening. He and his doctor agreed it was a matter of time; he had strong medicine to ease the attacks, but he would not give in to life-prolonging surgery.

So, he was surprised when he was suddenly left a widower. He was also, for the first time in forty-five years, relieved. And then guilty.

The dreams were sure proof of that guilt, he rationalized. Anyone might think so, at least in the beginning. But the dreams had taken on a bizarre turn since they began the week before. Monday. It was Monday last week. Monday night.

He noticed her walking into his dream. She was rigid and stiff, as in life – unbending, unyielding. And she stood there, far enough away so that he couldn't see her clearly. But he knew who she was. She was scanning the horizon, vacant in all directions ... straining to see, standing on tiptoe.

The second night, and all subsequent nights, he noticed that she came into his dream vision from his left. It was as if she were coming from ... and he marveled at the oddity of the thought ... the right hand of the Father—if he were also facing God. The second time she was closer, noticeably so. And she looked at him right from the start. Her eyes met his in recognition. He struggled awake. His chest was tight. He rose to find his medicine, and on the way back from the bathroom, opened the door to her room, half expecting to see her lying under the covers. But the bed was empty, and the room smelled vacant.

The third and fourth nights she watched him, studied him. She was also looking about as though for a safe path through the dreamscape. Little by little she approached.

When he came awake, it was with less assurance that guilt lay beneath his troubled sleep. He confessed the guilt, but the dream still was with him.

On the fifth night he could see the details of her lipstick. It was the mortician's work—far better than while she was alive. This time she beckoned him. Yes, she nodded. He was to come.

He was afraid. He reminded himself it was only a dream and ordered himself to wake. It took effort. And the chest pain had returned, more sharply.

The sixth night she was closer and gestured more severely. She wanted him to join her. He saw her lips move, and could imagine what she might be saying. But he heard nothing. The silence unnerved him. Again he fought himself awake, but at a cost. His breathing was ragged with strain. He had left his pills next to a glass of water on the nightstand. He reached for and then swallowed the tablets, spilling some of the water from his shaking hands. He dared not return to his slumber. Instead, he sat up all the rest of the night, thinking and praying. He remembered the tales, even in some of the early church teachings of the soul's flight from the body. There were those who thought that even if you had led a blameless and saintly life, at the very instant of death, it was possible for the dark forces to snatch the soul as it fled its earthly shelter.

All that was contrary to his latter-day protestant thinking, but still it was disturbing. As a result, his day went slowly. He felt ill. Sunday. His favorite day of the week. He attended services, returned to his modest supper, and spent much of the rest of the day reading. Shortly after sunset he considered his bed. He was weary, and though he dreaded what might come to him, he prepared to sleep. Nor did he neglect his prayers, including one for the eternal repose of her soul.

But neither did she rest on the seventh. She approached close enough so that he could have reached out and touched her.

Instead, she reached out to him. Horrified, he tried to escape her, but everywhere he turned, she stood before him.

There was no escape. Nor could he bring himself awake. He was trapped.

And the pain in his chest ... the burning. He must reach his pills.

No, there would be no pills. He would listen. She grasped his hand. There was no doubt that she was dead. She had the look of a well-preserved corpse. It was only the embalmer's art that kept her from appearing before him in decay. He felt his heart squeeze.

He was dying. She was taking him to death.

But here was no angel of mercy, no comforter. His last ally—death—was perverted in an instant. Instead of a joyous reunion with the saints, he now expected a much different welcome.

The pain faded; he could no longer feel his heart. He could no longer feel anything. But he could hear, he could see. And now he heard her words, words he'd so often used to comfort others.

But from her carmine mouth, the promise was damnation.

"I go to prepare a place for you," she intoned, parodying the Gospel of St. John. "And if I go and prepare a place for you, I will come again, and receive you unto myself; that where I am, there ye may be also."

His heaven would be hers. And for the first time in his dimming memory, she truly smiled, but slightly.

## To Be Forgotten

I knew that dying would be a big change. I had an idea that there would be a continuation. But I didn't know it would be like this, so enduring.

Some of what I thought would happen has indeed happened: the dying was painful. It was as though I passed through a fire. And then I was standing in the presence of those whom I had known and loved in life, those who had gone on before. And behind them, others whom I later learned were angels. Then came a face-to-face with God (I was kneeling in grateful adoration), a life review, a determination. There was all of that. And evidently, I made the cut, so I was not outright damned. That was a relief, for I had not led a perfectly blameless life.

And those loved ones who served as a welcoming committee? They remain near, and it's possible, even normal, to speak with them. There are now so very many nearly endless discussions. I think I have pretty well squared away all the misunderstandings with my parents, and even with all the evidence of being a real handful when I was growing up, they long ago forgave me. In the same manner, I like to think I have forgiven my own children. When at last they arrive, I will make sure they know that. And there have been others with whom I had been at odds over the years. We've had a chance to work out and through any number of issues.

I've had to apologize for many thoughtless remarks, cast unthinking into eternity.

But it's not entirely having to make right all I'd set askew.

One of the distinct advantages of this place is the ability to relive any moment from my life as if it were the first time, not merely a remembrance. Oh, yes. I have been able to relive the moment when I first met Mairi. Oh, golly, I was swept right off my feet. And I have relived her first shy smile to me again and again. (The fact the Mairi is not yet here is no impediment to my continued love for her.) My first car. My meeting of a new puppy. The birth of a son and a daughter. A career highlight that involved a large audience and a lot of applause. All those things were there to experience as I did the first time.

And then there were the things that I couldn't have anticipated: Time, time, time.

There is a lot of time here. So, it's not quite eternity, but it's right next door.

And there is the matter of how significant it is to be known. Or, more precisely, how important it is to be not-known.

That earthly preoccupation with fame and recognition? We all love to be recognized for what we've done (if we've done good things, mostly). From that, we seem to have a sense that we will live on for as long as we are remembered. And so, many of us have been concerned with our reputations. As it turns out, that is just so. As long as we are remembered we live on…here. That means that on any given day (or not day) you might encounter anyone famous from all of history with whom you'd like to speak.

And that's the problem. As long as you are remembered, you are here.

And there is a place beyond here which is where you WANT to go. That's heaven. This is…waiting. Maybe a kind of purgatory. Any remembrance of you must be purged. This means you must fade from any recollection. Even to the extent of all records. As long as you are in a book someplace you are stuck here. As long as there is a statue with your name on it, you are trapped in this not-quite-there.

This should not come as a surprise. We've been warned, for instance, in the Beatitudes that the poor in spirit inherit the kingdom of heaven. How much poorer can you be than forgotten? We also are cautioned against being too well thought of.

I have had a series of lengthy conversations with those who have been here for a long, long time.

Like a chat with Aristotle. (I know there would be those who would have been shocked to learn that a non-Christian would be in heaven. But he is, and so many others, too.)

Aristotle has been waiting and he knows he has a long time still to wait. So why not talk with those of us who thought his *Rhetoric* a masterwork? Or his *Politics*? He'd take it all back if he could, he's said. But he can't. And so, he has to wait until no one alive remembers him and there are no copies of his work left in print. It's gonna take forever. It's already been since the Fourth Century B.C. He held a hope during the so-called Dark Ages. But the monks found and saved his work, and then copied it out for all the libraries in the world. He was NOT slipping off into obscurity.

You might wonder what such an anointed mind would do with all us lesser thinkers hanging about, coming around to sit for a spell and talk. Better than you might expect. "Ari" has a lot of experience with patience. Every question that could be asked has been asked. Yet, he'll take another, or the same one for the millionth time. And he is not a frowning, forbidding presence. Like the rest of us, impatience has been seared. He is cheerful, probing, and willing to consider points of view that might seem antithetical.

In the process, what an education he has shared. By the very nature of this place, if I ask for a private conversation, I can have one. Or, if I want to be among the scholars of the Lyceum, I can mosey to the edge and over-listen. It is pleasant to hear and walk, to ask questions and understand answers, even if they are delivered in ancient Greek. We all comprehend. It's all *lingua franca.*

I am not likely to be here for seemingly all eternity; I was beloved by a few and as long as *they* live, I am here. But I can foresee a generation or two down the road that I will be able to move along.

There are a few who have never been here. Some who truly went beyond: Enoch, Elijah, and even a thief on a cross who was promised paradise "this Day."

Of all that are here, stillborns spend the briefest of times, merely a generation. It's wonderful to see them beginning to shimmer as they are forgotten. Then, with a snap, they vanish from here, presumably to be suddenly there, in the eternal presence of the Almighty. Next soonest forgotten are those who in life were the poor and hungry. Then those who were little noted.

I watched a maiden great-aunt of mine, Aunt Judith, go on. She had never been a seeker of attention, never had her name in the paper. In a local disaster, her birth and death records were consumed in a courthouse fire. (I'm not sure what happened to her Social Security records, but they must have vanished, too; some bureaucratic snafu.) She would show up at family functions and might chat with a few of us, but she seemingly was most content to sit and listen. Aside from recognizing her at family reunions, I rarely called her to mind. Here, I had a chance to amend my knowledge of her. She was a marvel. She had devoted her life to small acts of charity. Most of the recipients of her generosity didn't even know the source of their good fortune. For instance, I never knew in all my living years that my letter jacket in high school was from her. It just showed up one day in the post; no return address. But it was the right school colors, the right size. Just perfect. She was the giver. Even here she was hesitant to tell me of her gift. Now, her living memorialist, a niece (and someone who had known of much of the good that she had done; she had shopped for Judith and sometimes listened to others' hearts' desires), had entered the throes of a dementia. And then one day Aunt Judith was no longer remembered. I barely had time to wink at her when with a whoop she vanished. I am sure it was the sound of joy. Truly, the last shall be first and the first among us will be the last...to leave.

Many celebrated the transition of my great-aunt, even those who are likely to be here for what we'd call e-v-e-r. Dr. Albert Schweitzer played an organ recital in her honor. George Washington told me that he can only imagine what it's going to be like. As far as he's concerned, it's going to take something akin to the end of the world...every book will have to rot, all memorials will turn to dust. Civilization as we know it might have to grind to a halt. Only then will he be free of all the trappings that have so far constrained him, preventing him from walking into eternity. For those of us who are run-of-the-mill souls, we'll just have to wait and see. Paper records, photographic records (microfiche and the like), and digital records all will have to fade.

There are those who will be the last to leave. Christ, for instance. He is both here and NOT here; he promised us he would be with us to the end of the world no matter where we were. So, he is HERE, but he says he is everywhere and all at once. Meanwhile, the faithful flock to him and the others who have been deemed saints and such. And with infinite patience they tell us that the God-fire that is in them is the same God-fire that is in each of us. Yes, they will be here, perhaps even choosing to remain with us until it's lights out. But for the rest: line up and take a number. That we are here is enough for now.

But there will come a day.... We are promised that even time will have a stop. Then, at last, we will go on.

Until then, we must be about our business; for me this is not all Elysian Fields and milk and honey. ...I mean, maybe for some it is, but how much of that could I stand? My goal is to keep learning as much as possible; that is still of some value to me. Sometimes I am glad that I have at least a few lifetimes to acquire knowledge and think on it. I'm learning that many things could have been different.

If I could go back—like the rich man who was contending with Father Abraham concerning the beggar Lazarus—I would urge people to be less well thought of, to live content with small lives of little notice.

Better to be that impoverished soul at the gate of the rich man than to be the rich man.

And best of all to be forgotten.

## The Old Prescott

The building should have been down by now. Everything had been "arranged." The proper orders of condemnation had been secured and sent out to the lowest bidders. Getting this far had been an amazement; I did not expect that it would or could happen, but we had been assured by the voices of reason that it would be so.

There had been other, earlier efforts. But they had come to nothing. In part that was because the building was an unknown quantity said the city's engineers. (They were themselves an unknown quantity; there seem to be no records of their state-mandated engineering registrations and not a one of them was listed in the Engineering Department phone listings as a PE, a Professional Engineer; that's usually a measure of competency.) As far as the city's engineers were concerned, it had been easier to leave the building than demolish it. They equivocated, something unusual in engineers. But then, those were only the city's engineers. Outside consulting engineers (almost all of them PEs) were unanimous in their determination that the building had to come down in the interests of safety, health, and welfare.

Both groups DID agree on one thing: they could not predict exactly how the building might come down with blasting charges. The outside consulting engineers reported that the 17-story stone-clad edifice was old and likely in need of repair that would exceed the costs of new construction. Oh, yeah? I mean, they had not been given access to the interior of the structure to make their own first-hand determination, so they were more or less guessing and said as much in their reports. There were plenty of other buildings of a like age that were still standing straight and true, they acknowledged, but without building documents…and there were NONE, they could make no other recommendation in good conscience.

The Prescott looked as it always had. If it was falling apart, I couldn't note it from the pristine exterior.

The granite still brightly reflected the sun's rays. And while it was mostly plain on the lower floors—early Art Deco—about halfway up there was a radical change in style, most notably a series of gargoyles encircling each floor. I have seen pictures of them taken with telephoto lenses. They are mighty lifelike, crouched and seemingly ready to leap, tongues reaching halfway to their toes. I have studied those photos and—while it must be a trick of light—they seem to have different expressions from day to day.

But the damned thing still stands. Even the news media had entered the cause on both sides. The *News* argued against any idea such as the destruction of a fine old landmark. The *Free Press* editorialized that 17 floors was not that much, and either a parking structure or a taller building would add more value to the downtown. So, old and not especially architecturally significant buildings (even if they were oddly rendered in mixed style) should come down. But it remains a monument. Certainly, but to what?

Hmmmm.

Trailers bearing heavy equipment that had been summoned to be involved in the detonation and then the clearing away of the mess once the building was down still linger on the streets, lined up along the curbs with orange cones all around them. That's how near it came this time. The machines of destruction and removal are absolutely still as if even they can't believe that the plans have been changed; they sit stunned.

And so, drivers will come with their tractors in the next day or two and take away the trailered rigs, but for now they're under tight wraps. Armed guards roam day and night.

I am NOT an unbiased observer. I've always wanted the building down, felt that it needed to come down. I should know better than even to be surprised that the building will stay, but I had fervently and prayerfully entertained hope that it would be destroyed.

At the same time, I also fear any attempt to disturb it. Most of all I believe any effort will not—let me say, cannot—meet with success.

I have no doubt that tearing down Detroit's old Prescott building would be like disturbing a tomb, desecrating a grave. Certainly, it is my grandfather's last resting place (if you can call it rest). And he may have companions. If the building comes down, where will they go? (For that matter, where are they now corporally and spiritually? Are they really there?)

We believe—some of us at least—that Grandpa IS there.

Grandpa the dandy.

My grandmother, now long dead—perhaps mercifully in light of the razing scheme and its resultant uncertainty—agreed that no matter where Grandfather wound up, his overmindful self-importance would have been behind his eventual downfall, anyway.

As it was, he had the misfortune of standing next to the Prescott when his end came. The *Free Press* story reported he had been noted examining his tie in the reflection of polished granite when the laws of matter changed. He saw something intriguing in the glossy finish, reached toward it and was yanked through.

The police reports and the *News* account were a little more forthcoming. The observer was described as a young woman who said she saw the whole thing. She had stopped to admire something in a nearby shop window but had managed to keep a pretty steady bead on Grandpa. She had been noticing how nicely he was dressed and said she had seen him straighten his tie and tilt his Borsalino at a slightly more rakish angle. Then he put his nose close to the dark grey sparkling surface, as though looking for reflected imperfections in his face.

Grandpa then, she said, moved to touch the granite. She saw his fingers rest briefly on the surface before they melted through the stone's surface. He took them back in ready fashion, she said, and was trying to push himself away when a hand came out from the surface. And not just any hand. The newspaper account recorded her words: "It was awful, just awful. It was a monstrous hand."

At any rate, Grandpa wasn't fast enough. The hand found his collar, his tie, and his shirt front...and in he went. I bet he fought to get out, for I can remember as a young man being shown where he went in and, sure enough, there appeared an outline of a man with hands splayed against the inside surface, a kind of face with a mouth open in a scream. But that was a long time ago; the image has since faded. The *News* account bears testimony to being able to discern "the shocked sense of disbelief, the horror... the horror." Journalistic plagiarists!

The account continued with the report that the young lady who observed the transfer duly fainted.

She eventually revived, but not without consequence. She was later found to be with child and unmarried, so she might as well have fainted two or three times. (But more of that in a moment.) After the greater part of the commotion...a few weeks at least...my grandmother invited and then entertained the young lady at our kitchen table. She certainly wasn't welcomed into the parlor. Mother says it was Grandma's own version of the third degree.

Grandma learned all: Miss Dempster revealed with some self-aggrandizement that she had been watching Grandpa with a certain affection as he was the father of her budding child. And she was not positioned at a "nearby" window but standing right beside him. In fact, she smugly maintained, had she not loosed his arm so he could preen himself, she might have wound up on the "other side" as well. With a snort grandma assured her it was indeed a pity. With all the sordid details in hand, grandma dispatched her with little sympathy. I realize now that I might have—or have had—an aunt or uncle, maybe even cousins.

Grandma expressed little interest in the building or exactly what might have happened to grandpa. As far as she was concerned, he had deserted the family, even if insidiously abducted. It would have taken some years before he was declared dead, but there was no life insurance and so no rush. Grandma was left to go it alone. And she did. As a child I would ask her what had happened to him, and she would grow quiet for a time. At last, she'd come out with "He made his decision." I learned early not to ask for more; it caused her pain. My mother, grandma's daughter, had been a small girl watching and listening around corners when Miss Dempster took her seat in the kitchen. She was not at all shy talking about her father or walking past the Old Prescott. It was from her that I learned of the story and the ins and outs. And she thought it all bunk; her father had simply walked out of the life of the family, turning his back on them.

I wished I'd been able to ask Miss Dempster a few questions of my own, particularly in my teenage years, but no matter how hard I looked I never found her name listed in the phone book. Perhaps she had married. No one else has been able to give such close testimony, but I'm sure Grandpa's was not an isolated event…the disappearance, not the dalliance, although the latter would prove to be common enough.

Throughout my childhood, my mother would drag me with extra vehemence past the Prescott, no matter how hard I tried to pause there. I had to become a fast study. The shapes in the granite of the building always seemed to be changing. A pink, fleshy streak would show up one day, only to move to another place on the exterior the next time I walked past. Occasionally, figures would appear in fine detail. They did not appear as happy souls.

And once, when I was fifteen and not afraid of anything—and downtown on my own, I looked closely at the side of the building and saw there, swirling up through the flecks of grey granite, a face, an arm.

The devil, I thought, and stepped back just in time. A huge forefinger poked through the stone and wagged about as though lazily stirring the surface of a still pool.

It couldn't have been the devil, I later reasoned, because the skin was sparkling grey, like the stone cladding the building. Everybody in America knows that the devil is red. (That's what I had thought at the time.)

I haven't had another such encounter because I haven't since dared to closely inspect the surface of that old pile. Instead, I've fed my curiosity with crumbs, compiling from a distance as much about the building as I could. Calling it precious little is overstating it. I might as well be staring into the abyss. Nobody remembers anything concrete, stone, or steel. I've never met anyone who worked on the construction of the building…or even knew of anyone who knew anyone who worked on the building.

All I know is this: late in the spring of 1928 there occurred a week of freak weather. Downtown was socked in with solid fog. Everything normal stopped; people couldn't see five feet in front of their faces. I've read the papers of the day on microform; they're mighty slim, but then, not much was happening. The papers covered what they could, and even went so far as to report the rumors of the hubbub that spawned the Prescott.

The Prescott Building sits on the site of an old thoroughfare, then commonly called Paris Lane; one would have been hard pressed to find a more squalid and derelict neighborhood. Warehouses crouched on either side of the lane, their eaves impinging traffic. Paris Lane was ever a source of enterprise for the seedy element, the likes of whom furnished the metropolitan constabulary with no end of diversion.

During the heavy fog, residents of the surrounding blocks reported all manner of wrenching sounds. Some of them were quoted in stories saying they knew better than to venture too near the site. Distinguishable within the cacophony were the clankings of steel girders being hefted and positioned and the ringing peal of air hammers peening rivets. There also assailed the ears of any brave auditors the muffled oaths of a prodigious force of workmen, and the overriding sulfuric stench of diabolic industry.

When at last the fog cleared, the old buildings of Paris Lane were found demolished and heaped, pushed to the sides as if they'd been forced up and out by something coming up from beneath. And in the center, rising in fearful symmetry, stood the Prescott. It was the new Prescott then.

The three metropolitan newspapers remarked the edifice, competing in hyperbole, and told the odd tale of its sudden rising. There were certain questions raised then and in subsequent—but sporadic—inquiries (especially by outside engineers).

Questions like: Why are there no surviving blueprints on file of the Prescott building in the city archives? Where are the records of building permits and construction inspections? Who was the architect? What was the construction company? Who were the subcontractors? How did the building tie in with city gas, water, and electric lines?

Nor are there records of fire safety inspections. The city inspectors are somehow dissuaded from completing their duties and any outside investigators have been stopped at the door. Heaven only knows how many times the building has been condemned for noncompliance—those records seem to have vanished as well. But tearing down a skyscraper, even a small one—as I've seen—is no easy task.

And the building's management! The Prescott is owned by a phantom corporation. I have investigated, and every lead disappears. There has been a recurrent spokesman during all these years, one Archie Nemo. If math serves me right, he must be well over a hundred years old. But he doesn't look it. Maybe 45 or 50 in a tanned and fit George-Hamilton way. Startlingly blue eyes and carefully combed, acrylic hair. He showed up at events, meetings, anything where a public face has been or is required. The 1928 newspapers quoted him and described him as dapper. But of him otherwise, there is no trace. I have found no listed residence (it could be in the Prescott, I suppose), no voting records, no census results.

I am not quite sure what goes on inside the building. It seems mostly there are insurance companies, accountants, corporate lawyers according to the city directory, all with generic and vague names.

The place shows signs of intense activity. It's almost as if people swarm into the building for the beginning of the workday and reverse the process at night. No one saunters. Special night crews seem to take care of all maintenance. I have seen cleaning crews through the windows, moving from office to office and floor to floor. I have watched them from a diner across the street, sitting for hours nursing a coffee and a piece of apple pie. Maintenance trucks pull up and workers rush in, pushing carts, carrying toolboxes. They work like those possessed. But they are quiet as they go about their business. There are no shouts, very little conversation. In fact, I've seen no communication among them as I've watched.

I won't enter the building, but others have. A friend once walked in out of curiosity and described it as hushed. Even the elevators made no noise; he said there were no chimes when they arrived. He did not ascend in one of them, but he walked the main floor and then climbed the stairs to the mezzanine. He had been looking for a listing of the business interests in the building. Nope. The interior, he said, was probably all original…the rich woods and brasses, polished and shined. Time had seemingly left the building carefully curated. And the employees he encountered there were hushed as well. No one smiled, no one returned his greeting. He said, though, that he felt as if he were being closely watched. He would catch the sliding eyes of the armed guards as they looked away when he turned to them. It was as if they wanted him to note that he was under scrutiny.

I have even gone so far as to follow some of the leaving workers, to get close to them. Once, I intentionally bumped into a man in a brown suit who had come with others from the Prescott. I apologized. He looked at me without recognition as a fellow person and then just beetled off.

Where would these workers go when the building came down? IF the building came down.

Even with my hope for its destruction, I could never imagine the building coming down by only earthly means. In my mind's eye, I saw the slow arc of destruction, and the great wrecker's ball swinging cleanly against the building and bouncing off without so much as chipping the granite. And if crews had first removed the granite panels—surely, they're just facia— what would they find behind? Would the Prescott be hiding anything unusual, like Grandpa?

I call it Zeitgeist. That's what the building is, an evil ghost of the times, with a few relics like Grandpa mixed in for good measure.

Grandpa. For me it all comes back to him. I'd never missed my grandfather because I'd never met him; I was born decades after his encounter with the Prescott. Grandma assured me that I hadn't missed much, but the longing of my heart for a grandfather was strong. (There wasn't one on the other side of my family, either, by the time I came along, a late-in-life baby.)

And while I wished that he'd been a part of my life I didn't want to meet him in person; not, at least, this side of the grave. Or maybe the other side, either.

That's why I was worried; if the building were torn down, he might be released. Well, it *does* make some sort of sense, doesn't it? And THEN what?

On the one hand, that is why I was disturbed with the idea of the building's ruination.

On the other, I reasoned, it would be right to take down the building because, well, because it would be better than to leave it up. It is, for lack of a more specific term, tainted with the infernal. Just how evil I suppose heaven knows more surely than I.

So, when months ago I heard that some of the city council members had managed to put together a semblance of a quorum to follow up on the condemnation and demolition recommendations from the independent consultants, I had high hopes that the forces of heaven might strike a blow.

Not this time, it seems. Heaven can wait, even if I am impatient.

What galls me most is the manner by which the building was saved. The Prescott escaped destruction only after an eleventh hour move by the mayor. First, Hizzoner (that's fancy talk for the mayor, language my grandmother affected) cornered the contingent that was lobbying to level the building. He had heretofore kept his own counsel about the Prescott. But not anymore. He called the levelers in along with every favor he'd ever allowed out of his tight fists. The session was closed door in violation of the open meetings act, but the walls had ears, it seems. He gave them Hell—at least figuratively.

"I own your sorry asses," the mayor growled at them. "I've helped each and every one of you get where you are, and now it's time to make good on your debt to me. Either you help out here, or you're done. You will never have to worry about any further election or appointment."

What could they do, being mere mortals? They fled to their precincts only to deluge their constituency with message after message about preservation and historicity, the political poltroons trying to press all the hot buttons. And then Hizzoner made his case to the public in a news conference, with all the television cameras in town capturing his indignation that a group of muddle-headed progressives would even think of threatening the ageless magnificence of the Prescott. Outrageous! They had had—each and every one of them—a change of heart. It played well on television, which is how I saw it.

On hand was the ageless and blandly smiling Archie Nemo to acknowledge that the mayor had been most persuasive; he had convinced the Prescott management team to rent a whole floor to the city. There were questions from the local media. How much was all this going to cost us taxpayers? Mr. Nemo smiled and shook his head as if he missed the question. "The price?" one reporter shouted. Again, a shaken head.

That price leaked out, too, but later. Only about double the normal floor space for such an address. PLUS the city would pay for remodeling of its new offices! Would they take out permits? I wondered.

And just who should be housed there in such pomp and expense? The mayor himself. His office along with construction and other inspection offices, and public relations for the city! But of course! The whole damned bunch of obscurants! The mayor remarked he would move his own offices there simply to breathe in the feel of the grand old building. It had been, he assured the press, his favorite Detroit landmark. He felt at home there.

And I'll bet he did.

## Mrs. Kaiser's Radio

> *Be sober, be vigilant; because your adversary the devil, as a roaring lion, walketh about, seeking whom he may devour...*
> *—1 Peter 5:8*

"Little Jew boy. That's what you are ... a little Jew boy."

That's all Ms. Kaiser had to say, and I'd run from the room crying. Most of the time I'd head out of the house and behind the chicken coop. I wouldn't cry much, but I learned to nurse a grudge.

And I'd say to myself "I am not a little Jew boy—whatever that is."

Again, within a day, the fascination of watching this old woman would overpower the fear of her tongue. I'd creep back into the parlor where she'd be working her picture puzzle, humming along with her big old radio. The volume was always very loud, and the sound distorted. But it didn't matter to her. Occasionally she'd raise her voice from an open-mouthed hum, and she'd sing a few snatches of song in a harsh and unmusical croak.

I'd crawl in on hands and knees and behind her line of sight. And I'd do it especially when I knew she didn't want to be bothered. I'd watch her, her arm outstretched above the table, holding a colorful bit of sky, or a mill roof, or tree foliage.

Sooner or later, I would creep into the edge of her sight, and then she would spy me, turn to fully glare at me and fix me to the spot.

"Yes, sir, you must be a little Jew boy. Look at that hair. Look at that nose. That's what you are...no matter what your parents say. A Jew boy."

And she'd laugh her wheezing cackle. That cackle soon would indicate that her attention had moved back to her puzzle. She would breathe noisily and hum, always along with the radio, that great old Philco cathedral model, the tiny dial dimly shining from within. And she'd stay at her puzzle for hours.

My parents told me I was not a Jew boy, that calling someone a Jew boy was unkind. And we didn't use that language and should never call anyone that. There were people who were Jewish, and they practiced a religion different from our Episcopal faith; theirs was an older religion.

They told me not to cry when Mrs. Kaiser said things; she was an old lady. That made her deserving of respect. And besides, she was Aunt-Gram's friend. And Aunt-Gram was my friend.

But I didn't believe the relationship was transitive. Mrs. Kaiser was NOT my friend.

Every once in a while, she'd seem to forget herself and do something...nice. If she determined I had been very good, she would allow me to play with one of the toys of her youth, an iron bank that would work when a penny was placed on a tray held in the mouth of a small mechanical dog. The little hound ran on a ratcheted track, so that when the dog was pulled back and his tail was lifted, he'd stutter-step forward and deposit the penny into the bank itself. I would delight in putting the same penny in again and again. (I needed only the one for I'd long since learned the secret of emptying the bank.)

But those occasions were rare. Still, I thought the heavy little bank a wonder even though it was not much larger than a big box of kitchen matches.

> *...the righteous, and the wise, and their works, are in the hand of God: no man knoweth either love or hatred by all that is before them.*
> —Ecclesiastes 9:1

Every summer—and some Thanksgivings—we made the drive from Michigan to Slingerlands, just southwest of Albany. For one week in the summer—sometimes two—my father would come out to work and help Aunt-Gram on the farm. And my mother and I came with him. There were no lakeside or tourist-destination vacations for us, only serious physical labor for my father.

This working farm had made a living for my Aunt-Gram, her brothers, and even their mother, Carrie, for years, but not forever. They had bought and moved to the farm during the Great Depression. So, while the farm had been in the family all my life, Aunt-Gram and my parents could remember the days when they lived in the roughest part of Albany in an apartment on Pearl Street. Compared to that, the farm was an idyll.

Now it was Aunt-Gram who owned the house, who owned the barn, who owned the farm, who took care of the chickens, who tended the garden, who—with help—harvested the small crop of apples, and who allowed Mrs. Kaiser to stay with her for a modest fee.

It was Aunt-Gram who made the world move. It had been Aunt-Gram who raised my father when his mother died; his father couldn't care for him and his newborn sister.

My father showed his gratitude, his filial piety and love for his aunt, by laboring around the old place. He would paint the exterior of the house or reclaim some of the farmyard and former pastures from the tall weeds. He would work himself into a sweat day after day, attempting to make up for a year's absence in a matter of very long hours. My mother would tend to household chores as she was able. As a survivor of a polio epidemic some years before, there was much beyond her physical limit. She got off better than many, no iron lung, no braces. But still she needed to be careful not to overtax herself.

Mostly, I would tag along with my father during his exploits. I learned to wash windows, cultivate a garden, swing a scythe, and clean a chicken coop. I would work to the best of my strength and size until I was tired. And then my dad would send me either to play or to rest. I'd know that I'd helped at least a little with the chores.

Aunt-Gram would also take me with her when it came time to feed and water the chickens. I would draw water, scoop feed into the pail, scatter the scratch and call "Here chick, chick, chick." The hens would bound toward the bouncing grain, their wings half outstretched to give them added aerodynamic lift and increased speed. My job was to look for eggs in the straw-filled nests. I learned how to withdraw an egg from beneath a sitting hen, how not to flinch when I was pecked, and how to bluff the few roosters on the farm.

In the basement of the ancient farmhouse, I learned how to candle eggs, to look for cracks in the shells or the dread bloodspots that would make an egg unsellable. That made use of a homebuilt device of something like a paint can with an oval cut in the lid and wired with a light that was strong enough to shine through the egg. Then the eggs would be weighed on a little balance: small, medium, large, and extra-large. When an egg would slip to the floor, Aunt-Gram would help me clean up my mistake. She never scolded. But I knew she made her pocket money from the eggs, and I dropped very few. The dozens and dozens of eggs were stored away in four old monitor-top refrigerators, ready for the twice-weekly pickup. The compressors sat on top of the big white boxes; each looked like it was affixed with the turret on the USS Monitor, hence the name.

In the heat of the day, after the chores were done, when Aunt-Gram and my mother would be off shopping or visiting, while my father was sweating in the hot sun ... then I would creep in to take up my observation post in the parlor where Mrs. Kaiser worked her puzzles accompanied by the radio's blare.

She was dreadful. Catching her unawares, I would study her face, the deep-set eyes, sharp and vigilant, almost bird-like; the ears that hung with pendulous lobes—for all their mass, nearly useless; she shouted to hear herself and was always asking others to speak up and stop mumbling. Her mouth was nearly always open, her rasping breath whistling across her unnatural teeth, ill-fitting, always aslant and crusted. Saliva collected in her drooping bottom lip. She was forever daubing at it with various tissues. Withered chicken-skin flesh hung from above her elbows. She was shapeless. Even her ankles were like the butt ends of candles that had sat too long in the sun.

> *All things come alike to all: there is one event to the righteous, and to the wicked; to the good and to the clean, and to the unclean...*
> *—Ecclesiastes 9:2*

As I grew summer by summer, Mrs. Kaiser and I struck an uneasy balance...at least I struck an uneasy balance, for never once do I think I frightened or discommoded her. I had stopped crawling in to spy on her; I would just walk in and lean against a chair. Why? There was no television at the farm; Aunt-Gram had never taken a liking to it. So, frequently I would look in, just to see her still working over what might have been the same picture puzzle as the one she had been working on five years before.

She had stopped calling me Jew boy, but enjoyed telling me how evil I was and what a poor pupil I would have made under her tutelage.

"When I was teaching school, we knew how to take care of boys like you," she'd caw. "Yes, we did—" And she'd snap in a piece of her puzzle. "—We'd swat them until they learned manners."

Then she'd look at me directly.

"Manners are so important in a man," she would say. "That's one thing the late Mr. Kaiser could have taught you: how to be a good boy. Oh, my, he was so tall and straight, always proper."

Sometimes she would flop back into the slipcovered armchair and talk about him…about his business acumen or his athletic ability when he was younger. It almost always came back to what a good-looking man he was. I had seen a picture of him, the one she kept on her bedroom bureau. He was good looking in an old-fashioned way. Thinning hair over a narrow face, a smile that extended even to his eyes behind his wire-rimmed glasses.

Yes, it was a pity that he died so young, she'd lament. She'd been left poor. Dirt poor. Oh, she hadn't taught school when they were married. She turned to that only after…when she had a young son to raise.

She often would talk about that son, the ill-looking middle-aged man who rarely came to visit and then with liquor on his breath (this we understood from Aunt-Gram). Mrs. Kaiser would drone on about his high school honors and exploits. He had been a model student, she said, just a model student.

I saw him just once when he stopped by while we were visiting. To me he looked as old as his mother. I could not then distinguish between 50 and 80; both mother and son looked old, and the bags under his eyes were even more pronounced than hers.

While Mrs. Kaiser's departed husband and son could do no wrong by her accounting, I, on the other hand, could do almost no right. For the most part, she kept her ill feeling toward me between the two of us.

But there came an incident that remains one of the most unpleasant confrontations of my youth; for I was innocent of her accusation and yet could do nothing about it.

Mrs. Kaiser, as I intimated, had grown very deaf. She would brook no hint on the need for a hearing aid; at table my aunt would talk around her. (I often wondered what must have passed for conversation when we weren't there.)

I must have been about thirteen. The summer afternoon at the farm was especially lazy. Even my father had given up his chores in favor of a spell on the front porch. I sauntered into the parlor and stood watching Mrs. Kaiser at her puzzle.

"I think you have the piece for the sky that goes up here," I shouted, pointing at the puzzle table.

"Hunh?" she cawed, looking up at me with a sudden flush of anger. "No, no. That won't do. Now go away until you learn better."

I shrugged my shoulders and wandered out, mystified. I sat on the porch glider and tried to read a newspaper that my father had put aside, but I had not yet developed the habit. I gave up and wandered to the barn to range through the vacant stalls and to rummage through the long-disused tools. It was a place of the past. I could vaguely remember the horse, Dobbin, that had reigned in this barn, the once-motive force for all farm hauling. But he had died years before and been replaced by a little Ford 8N, now also gone. There was still some feed left in a disused feed bin, and I would watch as bugs scurried from the light when I lifted the heavy wooden cover. Opening the bin also released an aroma I would forever associate with the farm, rich in molasses and decay.

I had other memories of the farm. I remembered both my Uncle Frank and Uncle Bill well, really my great-uncles, Aunt-Gram's two older brothers. Uncle Bill had been frail and worked as an insurance clerk. He had little to do with farm chores and had died just after my earliest memories of the farm. But Uncle Frank had lived a few more years and had run the farm with Aunt-Gram. The barn had not forgotten his tread, or his genius with tools and animals. I was never afraid of his ghost, for the barn was always comforting.

The only place I would avoid on the entire farm was the hanging rack perhaps a hundred yards to the north of the barn, far beyond the big walnut tree; for it was there Uncle Frank would kill the turkeys. I remember watching him before Thanksgiving one year (we had traveled late) as he suspended them by their jaws, forcing their mouths open. Then, with a long and L-shaped razor-sharp knife, he'd slit the carotid artery, so easily reached on the inside of the throat. The birds would flap and whirl, sending bright red blood spurting and splattering. As the birds were dying, he'd then hang them upside down so all the blood would drain. I was always amazed that the grass grew normally beneath the turkey gibbet; there was no rank or unholy growth. But I would avoid the spot, nonetheless.

Inside the barn motes of dust caught the sun in the window above the workbench. I had busied myself in the barn, cleaning out and organizing tool drawers: all screwdrivers here, all hammers there. I jumped when my father yanked at the barn door. He was muttering under his breath, upset and red-faced.

"Come into the house, Sonny," he said. "Your mother and I need to talk with you."

Questions buzzed through my mind like nagging deerflies, but I followed. My mother met us on the back stoop. She grasped my arm above the elbow. She firmly steered me aside.

"Sonny, we need to talk with you about something Mrs. Kaiser says you said to her. I need to know: did you call her by her first name and then say something else...something bad?"

"No."

"We know she doesn't hear very well, but she says you called her Mabel and made some sort of obscene suggestion."

"Honest, Mom, I didn't. I wouldn't. All I was doing was trying to help her with her dumb puzzle."

"Well, we didn't think you'd say something bad, but when she complained we had to follow up. I'm sorry."

My father had been silent. I knew he didn't much like Mrs. Kaiser, and I realized that his red face was because he was angry with her, not me. He turned to my mother and spoke softly: "If it weren't for my aunt, I think I'd tell that old bat to drop dead."

My mother nodded and dropped her head. Mrs. Kaiser was in a state, she said, and demanded an apology.

"For what?" I asked. "For something I didn't do?"

"And if she doesn't get it," said my mother, "she'll make Aunt-Gram's life miserable. Sonny, I have a big favor to ask. I want you to apologize to Mrs. Kaiser for something you didn't do. I know it and your father knows it."

There was almost nothing I wouldn't do for my Aunt-Gram, but this? I'd have to pretend I'd been bad.

Mom said she realized it was like asking me to tell a lie. It WAS asking me to tell a lie.

But I'd do it. I'd do it for Aunt-Gram.

Mom came in with me. Dad stayed outside, still steeped. We shuffled in. The room was silent. For once the radio was off. Mrs. Kaiser finished putting in a piece on the picture. I saw it didn't match; she crinkled one of the lobes to make it fit. She looked up.

"Oh, you're back? Well, I thought you might be after I talked with your mother. I don't remember extending an invitation for you to call me by my Christian name. It's permissiveness," she said turning her stare on my mother. "And that other thing! I won't even dignify it by giving it a name."

I stepped forward.

"I'm sorry Mrs. Kaiser if I've done anything to make you angry. I wouldn't do it on purpose, believe me..."

I shouted my apology to make sure she'd hear it.

"You needn't bellow. I'm not deaf," she said, again turning to my mother. "Some youngsters just don't know how to behave. Now, I could teach him how to respect his elders."

With a frosty glare my mother left the room. Mrs. Kaiser turned back to me, not quite done.

"Sonny, plug in my radio. When your mother was dusting in here, she unplugged it."

I had to crawl between the bookcase and her chair to reach the outlet. As I lifted the plug from the floor, a book fell on my backside...at least I thought it was a book that had fallen until—my mission accomplished—I backed my way out and saw Mrs. Kaiser holding a raised volume, a thick *Reader's Digest* volume of condensed books. She had given me a thumping with it. She cackled.

I stood and stormed out, too mad to say anything.

I didn't return to Mrs. Kaiser and her parlor all the rest of our stay. But I could hear her radio, the incessant music oozing all around her.

Aunt-Gram noticed something wrong, but we did our best to hide it. By the time we'd left that late summer we'd pretty well made a game of avoiding Mrs. Kaiser.

> *This is an evil among all things that are done under the sun, that there is one event unto all... —Ecclesiastes 9:3*

The next year, while Aunt-Gram wasn't getting any younger, she still seemed light years more energetic than Mrs. Kaiser. The radio played on still. And I had learnt more about music, and I knew some of why I hated what she listened to. It was archaic popular music from the '30s and '40s, often performed for easy listening. I despised easy listening and found it instant-mashed-potato music; no lumps, no flavor. Simple and void.

But Mrs. Kaiser liked it ... so much, in fact, that she turned the old radio even louder. She was also growing more forgetful. She'd leave the radio blaring even when she went to bed. Aunt-Gram would have to come down from her bedroom to shut it off.

"I don't know how much longer I can look after Mabel," Aunt-Gram said as she stood at the kitchen table the early morning after we arrived. She then moved to retrieve a Freihofer's coffee cake from the cupboard (her second favorite, eclipsed only by their macaroons; but those were for afternoons). She served up three unreasonably large pieces and a smaller one for herself. She then poured fresh coffee and sat down.

"She doesn't hear a thing I say and then she complains because I never tell her things. I've told her and told her and told her to go to a hearing doctor, but no."

Mom asked if maybe her son could intervene. "Well," said Aunt-Gram. "He comes even less than he used to. He says it's because he can't talk with her, so she complains to me about him, too."

Aunt-Gram was caught in a quandary: "I promised her that she would always have a home here unless she wanted to move in with her son. But he says he can't take her."

I left my parents to the discussion and went out back and up the hill to the barn. I tugged at the great wooden doors to wheel them along the track. Only with all my strength could I get them to budge.

Lubrication was the answer. I found a tall fruit ladder, a can of grease and a rag and paint stick to apply it. Soon I was up at the track taking care of a decade or so of neglect. My efforts paid off, and I climbed down and ran the doors back and forth. I could move them one-handed.

    I was interested in all things mechanical and some electrical. I had discovered engines. Poking about in the barn, I determined that several old lawnmowers and an ancient Gravely garden tractor might benefit from my attention. Aunt-Gram had given me permission to fix anything that caught my eye. One of the lawnmowers simply needed the carburetor cleaned. That took maybe an hour. The other mower, an old two-cycle Lawn-Boy, demanded a new head gasket—an item not readily available. I would have to ask for a ride maybe into Slingerlands but more likely nearby Delmar. At the same time, I could pick up parts for the Gravely. From what I could see it needed a new fuel line and a sparkplug. Maybe then it would run. Oh, and fresh oil, too. I was determined to go and ask for ride.

    After the cool dark of the barn the bright sunlight was blinding. I had to squint even in the shade of the walnut tree. The heat had come up. Both my parents and Aunt-Gram were working in the garden; the two women labored around the gladioli, my father was hilling up potatoes.

    My mother agreed to drive me, on the condition that I knew where to get the part and that I'd fetch her purse. I'd have to make a phone call or two and we could be on the way.

    In the Yellow Pages I found a service dealer in Delmar...no more than a couple of miles. My call confirmed that the head gasket was in stock and at a price I could afford. I also decided to replace the magneto and the spark plug, just to give the mower every chance to start. They had those, too. And the plug for the Gravely and the fuel line and oil would be no problem. All that remained was to get the purse. And for that I'd need to go into the parlor.

    The radio was shouting something by the Ink Spots, "Glow, Little Glow Worm," or something equally noxious to a 14-year-old. Mrs. Kaiser was giving full vent to her rendition of the same piece, but out of tune and out of time. I spied my mother's purse on a chair across the room, and I hurried across the worn coiled rag rug. Somehow my foot caught, and I fell. As I fell, I reached out. As a result I brought down with me both the card table and Mrs. Kaiser's puzzle.

"Laws and stars," she screeched, blinked and pushed herself back into the chair. "You!" she growled. "Now, don't ya see, you've ruined my picture. Well, young man, you'll be busy enough for the next few hours picking up the pieces and... ."

"I'm sorry Mrs. Kaiser," I shouted over the blast of the radio. "I'll pick all this up. I tripped on the rug."

"On the what?" she queried.

I pointed to the rug. Already worn and ancient, it had been further damaged in my fall. Two of the coil loops stuck up out of the braiding.

"You've ruined your Aunt-Gram's favorite rug, too," she said warningly. "I'll bet there'll be a hidin' around here yet today; you just see if there isn't."

First, I put the table right and then dropped to my hands and knees picking up the puzzle pieces. Several large sections had miraculously survived intact, and I gave them special care. At the end, Perry Como was urging me to "Catch a Falling Star." I conceived an instant dislike for the song.

At least half an hour passed before I found and placed the last piece on the righted card table. Mrs. Kaiser was busy again. But she had time for another observation.

"It's a wonder you didn't dirty the pieces more with your hands," she observed. "Don't you ever wash? And before you go, put the rug right and tuck those loops back in. I'll tell your Aunt Gram what you've done, you can bet that. Now get!"

I started to leave but remembered my mother's purse and so returned, an action which freed Mrs. Kaiser's tongue still again.

"What are you doing with that? Men aren't supposed to play with purses; it makes them weak."

I glared at Mrs. Kaiser, thought of several things I wished I could have told her, and jammed my mother's purse under my arm like a football. Then I marched out of the room. I met my mother on the front porch.

"I was just coming in to see if you'd vanished," she said and paused. "Why, Sonny, what's wrong?"

I told her.

Forging peace was a matter of a few minutes' words with Aunt-Gram. Mother explained. I explained.

"Now, Mabel knows better than that," said Aunt-Gram. "That rug has been a danger for a long time. It's hers you know; she brought that with her when she moved in. I've been trying to throw it away for the longest time, but she won't hear of it. She won't let me change anything in there. It's not as if she owns the place."

We were able to pick up the mower parts, and I had the machines running before sunset. My parents beamed with pride. Aunt-Gram was almost as pleased as I was. At dinner that night, she tried to tell Mrs. Kaiser about the work I'd managed during the day. Whether she heard it or not, Mrs. Kaiser glared balefully at me from time to time, jabbing the air lightly in my direction with her fork. This time I didn't look away.

I managed to stay out of trouble during the rest of the trip, which turned out to be my last trip to the farm until I finished high school.

My parents continued to go every year, bringing home news of the farm, Aunt-Gram...and Mrs. Kaiser. They were concerned about the strain she put on Aunt-Gram. Strain or no strain, Aunt-Gram said she would never—NEVER—allow Mrs. Kaiser to be put away in a home, especially while she had some of her right mind. My father pointed out that it was more likely Aunt-Gram's health that would suffer.

Mom said Aunt-Gram was not above a little complaining, but she would also conclude with: "Poor thing. She can't help it."

And the radio? Always on, ever louder. Aunt-Gram said she was growing somewhat deaf, too, so the radio didn't bother her much. But it bothered the neighbors; Mr. Foote—usually the mildest of men—came to complain to my father one day when we were there. Both men knew there was nothing they could do.

> *...yea, also the heart of the sons of men is full of evil, and madness is in their heart while they live, and after that they go to the dead.*
> *—Ecclesiastes 9:3*

Mrs. Kaiser died with the radio roaring beside her. Aunt-Gram said she had been reading in the parlor where Mrs. Kaiser was sitting, as usual, working on a picture puzzle.

"She looked up at me and said 'Oh!' and she was gone," wrote Aunt-Gram. "I was so glad I could be with her at the end. The funeral was very nice, but very small, with only her son from her family. There were one or two others, but I didn't know them."

Mrs. Kaiser had died in the winter, just after the New Year. That same winter, Aunt-Gram came down with a cold that lingered. She had written that it was nothing that a little self-medicating wouldn't cure. A few days later Mr. Foote, the neighbor across the road who complained about Mrs. Kaiser's radio, called to let us know Aunt-Gram was in the Albany hospital with pneumonia, sick enough to be concerned about, but probably not at death's door. "Still," he said, "When you get to be that old, anything can become serious."

My parents called Aunt-Gram, made plans to go and see her. They flew to Albany and stayed overnight, spending most of their waking hours with Aunt-Gram.

She WAS on the mend. The doctor had been aware that her long-time boarder and friend had died.

He told my father, "She's tired. And she's sick. But she's not likely to die from this. The only reason she let us take her into the hospital was because with Mrs. Kaiser gone, she didn't have the same sense of purpose. I think she's mourning."

Even in grief, her constitution buoyed her. Aunt-Gram was discharged a day or so after my parents got home. Her correspondence resumed and her letters of the slowly dawning spring grew more and more confident and cheerful. So, my parents made plans to drive east in June, just as soon as I graduated from high school. This was the first time I was old enough to help with the driving. I looked at journeying with a new eye and as we approached the farm—even with my father at the wheel—I saw it all in detail: the bridge over the rail lines and the creek, the sinuous roadway that glided through the country and increeping suburban scape. Many of the small farms had given over to new subdivisions, a constant threat Aunt-Gram had bemoaned. And at last, the white farmhouse with Aunt-Gram waving from the porch. She hugged my parents and gave me a peck on the cheek; nothing gushy. After the car was unloaded, I was content to be quietly in the background. I was discovering pleasure in watching people. I watched Aunt Gram's aged hands plucking at the sleeves of her housedress in the joy of seeing her family. Her best housedress, too, I was sure.

Aunt-Gram was thinner than I remembered her, but aside from that, she seemed not much changed. She still had stories to tell, full of details of people's lives, things that happened, how people responded, and how they felt. She told my parents about the nurses at the hospital and how well they treated her. And she related some of what she had learned about their complicated lives.

Finally, over coffee, Aunt-Gram began talking about Mrs. Kaiser.

"I know that looking after her took a lot out of me," said Aunt-Gram. "But it also put a lot back in; she gave me a focus. I'm sorry now that at times I was irritated with her. She couldn't help it that what she did got on my nerves. And that radio! Well, it's been quiet enough around here since. Too quiet."

The next morning, though I rose at what I thought was an unreasonably early hour, Aunt-Gram still was up before me. I was old enough, I reasoned, to take over most of my father's chores, so I wanted to get a jump on the day...and (a little, I think) to leave him in the dust.

Aunt-Gram outlined chores she'd especially appreciate having completed. Finally she added: "And if you have time after that, maybe the barn... . Do you think you might be able to straighten the clutter out there? Nobody's done it since last you were here." Seasonal workers who came to tend the orchard had been lax about replacing and organizing tools, so there was something of a muddle.

After lunch...after I had mowed the yard and repaired a step on the back stoop, I was able to contemplate an afternoon in the cavernous barn. The barn was still my heart's delight. The smells were unchanged. The sounds were unchanged. True, there was a layer of dust on the workbench and some stray debris in the corners, but the building felt the same, a wonder to a teenager.

My father was working on a window in a downstairs bedroom of the house, replacing a cracked pane. Mom and Aunt-Gram were visiting in town. I could, I knew, plan on enjoying myself, working at my own pace. And, in fact, I was most comfortable working by myself, something I have reinforced since in the recognition that I am an introvert. But working alone did not mean working in silence. As a teenager I wanted music. I had brought no radio, but I was sure Aunt-Gram wouldn't mind if I borrowed one.

The nearest at hand was Mrs. Kaiser's.

I entered the parlor; there was a certain awe in approaching her chair. I was uneasy being in proximity to a place where someone had died. I bent down to unplug the radio and remembered the time Mrs. Kaiser delivered the book to my backside. The recollection still rankled.

I stood and considered the radio. When I was younger, all I had known was that it was an old and old-fashioned radio. In recent years I had begun to study all things electronica, and I understood that it was a Philco 90, a radio introduced in the early '30s that changed the broadcast world. It boasted nine tubes and both a volume and a tone control. It was fine furniture, too, with its gothic arches veneered in burled wood. It smacked of all things outdated. I lugged the small console from the room and was surprised at its heaviness.

I carried the radio up the hill to the barn. My arms were aching by the time I placed the radio near one of the few outlets along the workbench. I clicked on the power/volume knob and waited for the old tubes to warm up. There were a series of amplified clicks and then static.

But there was no music.

I began twirling the tuning knob in search of a station. The static continued, even though the needle moved along the dial. I gave the old Philco a tap with the flat of my hand, judging that I may have loosened tubes in my cartage. Then, too, I thought, it might be as likely that some of the old tubes, sitting unused, may have disintegrated...or maybe they just took a long time warming up. I left the radio on while I started cleaning.

It was some time before I became conscious of a faint susurration. At first, I thought the rustlings were caused by the prowlings of one of the periodic cats Aunt-Gram took in. I looked up and followed the sound with my ears. I realized the noise was coming from the radio.

Wiping my grimy hands on my jeans, I walked toward it.

I recognized the pattern of a voice. I tuned the dial. No change in clarity, although the sounds grew just a little louder. I had given up and turned to walk back to the bench when I first heard the voice clearly enough to understand it.

"... Cordy ... Cordy ...?"

That was Aunt-Gram's given name, Cordelia. I spun around.

"... Cordy, where are you? Cordy ... please. Where are you?"

I knew that voice. Mrs. Kaiser's radio...Mrs. Kaiser's voice. The loathsome voice. I moved toward it.

"...Cordy. It's been so dark. Nothing, just nothing. And then this. Cordy, are you there? Say something to me."

I grasped the knob to turn off the radio when Mrs. Kaiser's voice screeched: "No! Don't! Don't close it. Please? *Please!*"

I snatched my hand back. The voice from the radio had degenerated into pleadings and keening, the static returned in waves. I backed away. My stomach felt like it had filled with hot oil and burst, filling my feet. I backed to the open door and then turned and ran. Not to the house; instead, I went farther still up the hill away from the house and the barn. I slowed to a brisk walk through the orchard and came at last to rest at a brush pile. This was the most eerie spot on the farm, for not only were there piled brush and tree limbs from the orchard, but there were remnants of furniture: the pigeonholes from an old and rotted desk, a rusted wash tub, and the remains of an ancient horse-drawn wagon. In the tangle of the blackberry vines I sat on the seat of the wagon. Hornets, disturbed from their nests buzzed about me, passively curious. One landed on my pant leg, but I let it crawl.

Mrs. Kaiser was in the radio. She was there, and she knew I could control whether she reached the living world. She wasn't dead. But I knew she wasn't alive. The dread of her haunting left me cold to my bones.

I realized that even afraid, I had questions. If she knew I was going to turn off the radio, why didn't she know who I was? Could she hear me if I spoke? Would she know me? And what could she do to me if she did?

And this wasn't exactly something I could tell my parents about. This was up to me.

It took some time, but I realized I had to go back into the barn. I had left the lights burning, and I had work to do. But not with the radio on.

I worked up the courage to walk back to the barn. I paused once by the long unused and decaying turkey gibbet and again under the black walnut tree. From under the tree, I could hear the sound of Mrs. Kaiser's voice raised in mumbling and complaint from within the barn.

I walked in and grabbed the first tool I could find, a garden rake.

"Who's there?" asked the disembodied voice.

"Me, Mrs. Kaiser. Sonny."

"Who? Sonny? I don't kn.... Sonny? *Little* Sonny?"

"I'm not so little any more, Mrs. Kaiser."

"Has it been long? I don't know. There's no time here."

"Where are you Mrs. Kaiser? I mean, I know you're in the radio, but you're someplace else too. Where is that?"

"It's dark. Awfully dark. I'm near the only place where there's a little light, like a pinhole in a card. That's how I found you. I saw the dim light. I can't see out, just that it's light here. I don't know. I'm frightened." Her voice dropped to a familiar mumble before she cleared her throat and resumed. "There's something else here. Something, somewhere. It's not good. No. Not good."

I wanted to silence her. I again reached out toward the switch when she screeched.

"Don't, Sonny!" Her voice softened, sickeningly sweet. "Don't turn it off. What do you want me to do? I'll do anything...anything I can, but don't turn it off. Just tell me.

"I want you to be quiet," I said. "I don't want to hear you say another word."

The radio fell silent except for the occasional crackle of static. I hoisted myself up on the workbench and sat watching the radio. The dial light of the old Philco pulsated from its accustomed yellow to a reddish brown. There was something...attractive...about watching it, something that wanted to draw me in. And something in me that made me want to go. I could....

And then I remembered that silently waiting was Mrs. Kaiser. Waiting and waiting. And I grew angry. With a shake of my head, I managed to look away.

I knew Mrs. Kaiser would have to go...even if that meant she went forever. Determined, I walked toward the radio. At the last I veered away and grasped the plug at the socket.

"Nooooo...," she wailed as I pulled. The radio gave out a sharp "pop" and was dead. I stood holding the cord, shaky and sick.

> *For to him that is joined to all the living there is hope: for a living dog is better than a dead lion.*
> *—Ecclesiastes 9:4*

When I got back to the house, Aunt-Gram and Mom had just returned. They hailed me to come and help with packages.

"I can tell Sonny's been working," Aunt-Gram said to my mother. "He's dripping wet." She turned to me. "You ought to go down to the creek and cool off. Or do you want a soda? There's 'cold' in the refrigerator. Ginger ale?"

I nodded, so with our arms filled with bags, we trooped up the back steps and into the kitchen.

Aunt-Gram poured three glasses of Canada Dry ginger ale, dropped in an ice cube each and set them on the kitchen table. I dropped into a chair, still trembling internally, and watched as she put away the groceries. I was struck that everything in the kitchen was immaculate. The old, scarred linoleum was nonetheless clean. The sun caught the jar of kitchen spoons that sat on the table. I had always been fascinated that in a house where order was the rule, the kitchen spoons were always left out; a carryover from the days when there had been so many making a living on the farm, and everybody sweetened their coffee with many spoons of sugar.

She shuffled a chair, adjusted the curtains, and put away the shopping bags. Finally she came to sit down. My mother had gone upstairs to her bedroom to change out of her shopping clothes.

"Aunt-Gram, do you believe in heaven? I mean, is that where Mrs. Kaiser is?"

She looked at me a long time before she answered. "You've always been a serious boy. And this is a serious question."

"I believe in a heaven. I think it's there in the here and now, and that's where we go when we die," she said and paused. "It's easier to believe if people have lived good lives. Otherwise, some say they go to hell. But I believe a lot of people we might think of as 'bad' people get into heaven, too. Christ died for our sins, you know, and that means that a lot of us who otherwise wouldn't make it are let in without having to pay the full price. I'm sure that those of us who love the Lord will meet again on the other side of the grave.

"As for whether I'll see Mabel again, I'm just not sure. I felt responsible for her in a way. But for as long as she lived here, I could never get her to go to church."

Aunt-Gram stood up again and began to fuss with the curtains over the table.

"Sometimes she'd talk right through grace at the table. And when the reverend would come, she'd start muttering under her breath, giving him nasty looks until he'd leave the room. He learned to stay out of her way, and we'd talk in the kitchen.

"But I'd guess that she's paid the price if there were a price to be paid. I still pray for her every night."

She smiled wistfully at me.

"You know they say the old must die and the young may. And I believe that what comes after is really the important part. I hope I'll see her again and maybe then we can sort it all out."

Before dinner, I crept out to the barn again. I didn't plan to stay long; certainly, I didn't want to be there after sunset. My understanding was limited, but I thought that somehow, even after death, that I had something of Mrs. Kaiser in a box. And as I disliked her in life, I positively loathed her in death.

> *For the living know that they shall die: but the dead know not any thing, neither have they any more a reward; for the memory of them is forgotten.*
> *—Ecclesiastes 9:5*

I switched off the radio before I plugged it in; I wanted some control when I'd hear her again. Then I switched on the volume knob and sat back to wait for the tubes to warm up. As the rush of static filled the room, so did Mrs. Kaiser's voice: "...back. I stayed right here where the hole had been. I knew you'd come back, Sonny. How long was it? I can't tell here. I've been so afraid."

"I was gone for a couple hours," I said. "Or did you want to know how long it's been since you died?"

"Died? Died—" and with a dawning realization "—of course I died. I remember I was going to take a nap one minute, and the next I was squeezed out of my body, just

squeezed. Oh, the pain! And then this. How long have I been here?"

"Six months."

"Six months. That doesn't mean anything anymore."

"Are you alone there?"

"I don't think so. I think there might be some others like me, but I haven't found them. And there's something else here. A sort of bird."

"A bird?"

"No! Birds. They fly, all in the dark. I don't think they can see, and I don't suppose they can smell or hear, but they flap around—they come in a flock. They run into each other. I think I heard them get somebody or something once. I heard the flapping of the wings and then screams, terrible screams. And I know that they want me."

Her voice had lost much of its querulousness. She was pathetically grateful for this lifeline.

"It sure doesn't sound like you're in heaven," I said. "But is it hell? I mean, are there any flames or stuff like that?"

"Maybe it's hell," she whispered. "Maybe Cordy was right."

Mrs. Kaiser broke off, and I heard her begin to quietly weep.

I reached out to turn off the radio. This time there was no shriek, just a word "... please?"

I turned her off anyway, unplugged the radio, and left the barn, sliding the door shut and fastening the padlock on its hasp. Back in the house, I picked my way through dinner, and shunning even reading, went to bed.

My dreams that night were full of wet flapping things. In absolute blackness. They were looking for me. If they found me, I knew they would tear me apart. In their search they would fly into each other, fall sickeningly to the ground and squabble. All the while they would croak something that sounded like, "Eat. Eat. Eat."

I awoke shortly before dawn to the flapping of a pull-down blind before a partly opened window. It knocked gently against the frame. I looked out to see a halo of moist air around the yard light. All else was in dark. It had been raining and everything was wet. I dressed rapidly, sliding into my pair of dirty blue jeans, and tiptoed downstairs. Even Aunt-Gram was still asleep.

I took the key ring for the barn and crept out the back door. The rain had diminished to a mist. From the stoop, I surveyed the barely visible barn, swathed in mist. Beyond, up the hill, the orchard was visible shrouded in white. The tree trunks were only vague suggestions of dark sentinels.

I set my shoulders against the wet and climbed down the steps. As I walked, I jammed my hands in my pockets. With each step up the hill, I vacillated. At the door, I turned around to look at the farmhouse. I leaned against the barn, trying to think, trying to draw some kind of strength from this fortress.

Destruction would be best, I thought finally. The radio is sick—sick with Mrs. Kaiser.

But what would happen to her? Was she real? Certainly she was real. I had heard her. I knew the voice. If I destroyed the radio would the birds get her then? I shuddered at my dream-image of the devourers. I could imagine that such an end would not be easy.

I unlocked the padlock, and went in. The dark was moist, cool. I found the light switch. Its click was like the report of a shotgun in the stillness.

The radio was right where I left it, unplugged. If I were to destroy it, I'd have to carry it. And to carry it, I'd have to embrace it. Hesitantly, I lifted.

I edged my way over the barn threshold, and down the slight incline, accustoming myself to my new center of gravity.

My destination was the junk pile in the orchard. The radio wouldn't last long there, I reckoned, especially if it received one or two solid blows from a stout stick of apple wood.

The mist swirled before me as I rounded the end of the barn and turned slightly away from the direction of the house. Just to my left what I thought was a tree trunk moved. I nearly dropped my ghastly burden.

Whatever it was moved toward me through the fog.

Was this Mrs. Kaiser escaped from her death? Oh, God!

"Sonny?"

Aunt-Gram! My knees went limp and sweat broke out on my forehead.

Aunt-Gram walked toward me, her face taking on clarity as she neared. Her robe was cinched over her nightdress. She had tossed on the overshoes she routinely left on the porch for walking in the wet grass.

"I heard you leave the house, and I wondered if there was something wrong. ...If maybe you heard somebody out here prowling about."

She studied me.

"What are you doing with Mabel's radio?" she demanded. "And at this hour?"

I shifted my load. "If you really want to know...."

"I do."

"Then let me put this back in the barn; I took it there yesterday when I was doing the cleaning. I didn't think you'd mind."

She followed slightly behind me as I retraced my steps. I put the radio just inside the door on an overturned barrel. The cord just reached an outlet. I plugged it in and switched it on, half expecting the radio now to work normally.

But no. There was the static. Aunt-Gram looked from me to the radio and back again. "So?"

Mrs. Kaiser's voice came faintly seeking. "...Sonny? Are you there?"

"I'm here Mrs. Kaiser," I replied, all the while keeping my gaze on Aunt-Gram. I felt a new courage with her in the room.

Aunt-Gram backed into an upended crate and plopped down. Her face turned to mine, full of questions.

The voice came again from the radio: "They almost got me. I was never so afraid in my life. One of them touched me; or it felt like it. Cold...slimy. And then the light came, just in time. Please, don't turn it off again, not ever. Next time they'll get me for sure. They know I'm here."

Aunt-Gram stood and crept forward, looking first at me and then the radio. She reached out to touch it but drew back. She whispered: "She's in there?"

I nodded. And we waited.

"What's going on?" Mrs. Kaiser demanded. "Sonny, who's there with you? I heard somebody."

"Never mind, Mrs. Kaiser," I said, motioning Aunt-Gram to the door. "I'm going away for a little while, but I'll leave the radio on. I'll be back."

"No. Don't leave! They might come again if you're gone. Don't go."

But I was already out the door with Aunt-Gram. We moved under the black walnut. She turned to me. "Leave the radio on and come with me to the house."

We walked in silence. Stiffly, she climbed the back steps. She shucked her boots and found her slippers just inside the back door.

Once inside the kitchen, she stood by a chair, drumming her fingers, absent-mindedly. Abruptly she broke off and began bustling to fill the coffee pot.

"I can see why you were taking the radio...somewhere. Tell me about how you first heard Mabel. What happened?"

I explained the events that led up to her first words from the radio.

And then I ended resolutely: "We have to destroy it."

"Hmm. But then what would happen to Mabel?"

We sat in silence as the coffee finished perking. I stood and poured two cups. Aunt-Gram stirred some sugar into her coffee in direct violation of her doctor's latest orders.

"And who are 'they' who almost 'got' her."

I explained about the birds. I even told her my dream.

"No, I don't think we should demolish the radio," said Aunt-Gram after a long pause. "She's trapped where she is. Maybe like a purgatory...a waiting place. And if we ruin the radio, she might never get out."

I waited and watched Aunt-Gram think her way through all she'd seen and heard.

At last: "I'll come with you back to the barn. I want to talk with her. And then I want you to carry the radio back to the house...here. To the kitchen."

"But, Aunt-Gram, you've been so sick. Do you really want to bring her back into the house. She almost killed you when she was alive. What's she going to do now that she's dead?"

Aunt-Gram looked at me over her coffee cup. "She might kill me, but she can't hurt me." She gave the faintest suggestion of a two-eyed wink and a smile.

The sun was just rising and beginning its struggle with the mist as we walked up to the barn.

"Promises to be a hot day," observed Aunt-Gram. "A real scorcher. I'll want to do a little gardening before too much longer."

Mrs. Kaiser heard our approach.

"Sonny, who's with you? And don't try to lie to me; I have perfectly good ears."

Aunt-Gram stepped between me and the radio.

"It's Cordy, Mabel. Sonny talked with me this morning. Are you all right?"

"Cordy, I'm afraid it's hell. I'm dead and this is hell. I'm so glad you came." Mrs. Kaiser broke into loud sobs and wails. Perhaps, I thought, the noise will attract the birds. Aunt-Gram was making comforting noises and had gone so far as to lightly stroke the case.

"We're going to have to unplug the radio for a few minutes, dear," said Aunt-Gram. "That's so we can move you back into the house. Did you know you were in the barn?"

No, Mrs. Kaiser did not know, nor was she pleased about the prospect of going back into the darkness. But Aunt-Gram could be persuasive and reassuring. Mrs. Kaiser made her promise four or five times that the radio wouldn't be shut off for long.

"All right. Bye-bye," said Aunt-Gram shutting off the radio as if she were ringing off the phone.

I unplugged and hefted the radio for its return trip to the house. As Aunt-Gram opened the screen door for me she fixed me with one of her cautionary gazes.

"It wouldn't do to tell your parents about this," she said. "For now, I think we better keep this between us."

I nodded.

Once again in the kitchen, Aunt-Gram busily set about sliding the coffee cups on the oilskin tablecloth, making room.

I plugged in the radio. Aunt-Gram turned it on and started talking even before the tubes had warmed up. "Now we're back in the kitchen. Oh, it's still before sunup, but it's going to be bright today, just the kind of day you love."

"Cordy? I was so afraid again. I've missed you so much. And I've had time to think about what you used to say. About dying and heaven and hell. And I'm in hell now. Oh, God!"

"I don't think it's hell. If it were, you probably wouldn't be able to talk to me. You'd just suffer. Are you in pain?"

"No, but I'm afraid. I'm afraid of the dark...and of them."

"Well, I think it's more likely that you're in a place like a limbo or a purgatory ... something the Catholics believe in. You were a Catholic when you were a little girl, weren't you?"

"Why, laws, yes. You know I've told you that before. But I never churched after I grew up and got married. Mr. Kaiser feared nobody...not even God, he said. So we never went to a church."

"I think you're in a purgatory," said Aunt-Gram. "That might mean you can get out sometime."

"Unless she's a ghost or some kind of evil spirit," I interjected in a whisper.

Evidently, she was no longer post deaf: "Sonny, I'm no ghost." Her voice had taken on the sharpish edge I remembered. I shivered. Aunt-Gram had caught my involuntary motion. She shook her head and looked puzzled.

"Well, she seems truly good and stuck where she is," she said turning to me. "I suppose it's my duty to help her get out of there if I can."

I motioned with my finger for Aunt-Gram to follow me into the dining room.

"Where are you going, Cordy?"

Aunt-Gram replied. "We'll be back. Don't fret; we'll leave the radio on."

When we were out of what I thought might be Mrs. Kaiser's range, I turned to face Aunt-Gram.

"Aunt-Gram, let me smash the radio. This is no good. It's not right. If I bust up that radio, then maybe she'll get out of purgatory. Let me do it now."

"You'll do no such thing. Mabel needs me and I'm not going to desert her. It wouldn't be...Christian."

I was less worried about it being Christian than paying attention to my sense of danger.

"She might suck you in there with her."

"Well, there are worse things than death," said Aunt-Gram defiantly.

"And what would Mom and Dad say?" This was my only power card.

"If they find out it will only be because a certain young man couldn't keep a secret."

Under Aunt-Gram's stern stare, I walked out of the dining room, through the living room, and onto the front porch. I flopped down on the rusty glider. In a few minutes I heard the screen door open and then I was not altogether unhappy to find my father soon sitting next to me in a spring rocker. The early morning was his favorite time, and he relished just sitting and looking at the new day. There was a cup of coffee in his hands. He looked up and smiled.

"What are YOU doing up so early?"

I shrugged.

"Will you be sorry to leave tomorrow, Sonny?" he asked in all simplicity.

I frowned. "I didn't get everything done," I said. "There's still—stuff to be done in the barn. And...."

"Believe me, I know," said my father. "But you never can get caught up here. It always seems as if there are just too many things that demand your attention."

It was my turn to smile, but sourly. I suppose that I managed to discourage conversation in a way that only teenagers can, and I rocked back and forth in the glider.

The day was full enough with last-minute tasks. Every time I walked through the kitchen, I noted the radio was still on and Aunt-Gram was hovering. But there was no sound that I heard from Mrs. Kaiser.

That night's dinner was somber. Mom and Dad both were worried about leaving Aunt-Gram. She certainly was better, but she looked a little pale and strained. They were also worried, I knew, because they thought our visit might have been the cause for that strain; having company is lots of work. They didn't know the half of it. I kept sneaking glances at Aunt-Gram.

"Why so glum, Sonny?" My mother had been watching me.

"Oh, nothing, I guess. I was just thinking."

Aunt-Gram shot me a warning look.

I wanted badly to talk with Aunt-Gram before we left, but there just wasn't time. For her part, I don't think she wanted a conversation; she stayed busy near my parents.

And when we finally pulled away from the farm the next morning, I felt that everything was wrong: Mrs. Kaiser was still—I was sure—on or in the radio; Aunt-Gram was going to do something—anything—to help her; my parents had begun "discussing" about driving straight through or stopping overnight. It had all gone wrong. I felt lonesome for something I couldn't pinpoint. When I wasn't driving, I tried to sleep all the way back to Michigan.

And back home, everything looked a little less real and certainly a great deal less interesting. I tried to talk about Mrs. Kaiser's radio with a few friends and found that I couldn't even do that.

As the weeks passed, the poignancy faded, and summer began to exert its charm. July was hot and damp, sweltering and muggy. I had found yard work for the summer and was making a tidy pile. Soon I'd have enough money for my own mower; the rest would go in my college fund. In the second week of August, all my plans changed as I had feared they might. We'd have to travel to New York again.

At the center of the trip was—of course—Aunt-Gram. She was ill again and wanted to see us. Her recovery had been short-lived, she told my father, and she feared that she hadn't much longer; she was wearing out, she said. She also made a point of asking for me to come along.

"But, Dad!"

"I'm asking you, as a favor to me."

I knew I couldn't turn him down.

"You'll need to pack for a while…a week or maybe two. And I may have to take a leave from work."

He also consulted Aunt-Gram's doctor. Yes, she was failing. Her heart? A little worse than average, but at her age, there was no telling.

> *For man also knoweth not his time: as the fishes that are taken in an evil net, and as the birds that are caught in the snare; so are the sons of men snared in an evil time, when it falleth suddenly upon them.*
> —Ecclesiastes 9:12

We were driving a powder-blue 1964 Chrysler Newport. I was allowed to drive much of the way back to New York. I watched my speed; those were the days before cruise control. The car was a joy and really handled well. With 361 cubic inches, it was no dog.

Watching the road, I still had time to think about what I was heading toward. My work might well be different from my parents.

We planned our trip so that we'd arrive in midmorning. When we pulled up to the house, for the first time in my life, Aunt-Gram did not come out to greet us. Not even the lace curtains of the parlor twitched. My father rapidly strode to the front door. The hollow sound of his feet on the porch found an echo within me. The door was locked. He cast a worried glance at us and started around for the never-locked back door.

My mother sighed when my father came through the house and out the front door. He was smiling and nodding his head to us. I noticed that his smile seemed fixed...as though he were smiling for someone else's benefit.

He was. Aunt-Gram was propped up on a daybed in the living room. She had dozed off and missed our arrival. She hadn't even heard my father at the front door. She now looked confused, unsure. She took in my parents and then settled her eyes on me.

"Sonny. Good. Now I can finish." She managed a faint smile and let her head fall back. She was instantly asleep. She was thinner. Her breath came softly, regularly, but weakly. Her color was ashen; there was no trace of the ruddy health I had remembered.

We knew that her neighbor across the road, Mrs. Foote, had been tending her. (It had been Mrs. Foote's husband who had complained about the noise of Mrs. Kaiser's radio.) She had been watching for us and within minutes was at the house.

"I locked the front door," she said wiping her hands on her apron, "because I thought just anybody could come in. I left the back open as per usual. I didn't see you drive up. I've been here morning and night. She don't look good, does she?"

She ducked in to check supplies in the refrigerator. She checked the commode, and then ducked out again, promising to be back in the afternoon.

After our luggage was stowed in the bedrooms, I stole down the backstairs to the kitchen. The dial on the old Philco was lit, but the volume was turned down. I twisted the knob slowly and as Mrs. Kaiser's voice grew louder realized that it was now working.

"Soon, Cordy, soon. I feel the prayers working."

The voice was stronger, smoother, deeper. There was no fear even when I spoke.

"Mrs. Kaiser, Aunt-Gram's dying."

"Sonny, is that you? Dying you say? Hunh! Oh, she won't die. You'll see."

And she wouldn't say another word. I didn't turn off the radio. Perhaps if I had, things would have been different. I reasoned that this was Aunt-Gram's house; if she wanted the radio on, it would stay on. Even that radio.

Later in the afternoon, I was sitting with Aunt-Gram, reading a magazine. She struggled awake, as though a swimmer coming up from the depths and hungering for air.

When her eyes finally fluttered open, there was a look of panic, confusion. She looked around the room, comforted at her familiar surroundings. She saw me and started. And then she recognized me.

"Sonny, I'm glad you've come. I have to tell you about the radio. Mabel is trapped. I've been praying for her night and day, and she's still trapped. I don't know any more. Maybe it's worse than I think. She says it's helping, that I have to pray more, have to talk with her more. But I'm not sure. The more I pray for her, the weaker I get."

She paused, closed her eyes, and rested. Her breathing, though steadier and more relaxed, did not deepen into sleep respiration. At last she looked at me again.

"Was I gone long? No?" I shook my head. "Each time I get a little farther away. That's part of it, part of dying.

"I don't mind dying, really. We all have to. But still I hold on, at least a little bit...burning to the socket."

She looked at me, this time with much the same intensity I remembered.

"I don't know if I did the right thing by stopping you when you were going to destroy the radio. I just don't know.... I'd just as soon fight with the birds as be trapped inside that box."

Even I could sense that Aunt-Gram was changing, preparing. My parents came in to sit with her, and when she was awake, she'd talk softly and slowly, regressing more and more into days of the past, days full of her parents, her brothers, and her long-dead husband (she'd been widowed after only a few years of marriage).

For the next three days, she ranged among sleep, events fifty years before, and the present. With the lightest of treads, she would hop through the years, calling my mother her mother, talking respectfully as a good daughter ought. Then, with a shake of her head, she would jump to her deathbed, leaving instructions on the disposition of her estate; the chairs and dining room table had to go to Cousin Ethel, the good silver to her niece, Ruth.

For all its usual attendant dread, her death was peaceful. She died at 9 a.m. on Thursday. She had rallied, her mind clear as a bell. Her doctor had just been in again to confirm that she was physically just slowing down. She was in no pain, looked at us and said "Oh, my dears," and just slipped away, her eyes half closing, her jaw parting slightly.

Mom, who had been stroking her hand, held it, and let the tears run down her face. My father turned to me in silent anguish. This was the loss of his dearest family.

This was my first death. I bolted from the room and ran into the kitchen. The radio was still on but low. As I turned the volume knob, the swell of Mrs. Kaiser's laughter danced round the room. I listened to her wheezing cackle for perhaps a minute before I heard the other voice.

It was Aunt-Gram: "You're not Mabel!" She was cut off by more laughter...Mrs. Kaiser's voice, but at the same time, another deeper voice of glee as well. "Oh, Cordy! I've been waiting so long, so long, now. But here you are!" And the sound of birds, great flapping birds.

Then Aunt-Gram shouted a final plea: "Sonny, smash the radio. Kill it."

I grasped the radio, the plug being pulled out in my dash for the door. But that didn't stop the sound coming from it. I felt it writhe in my grasp. The screen sprang away from me as I charged through the door. I ran into the stoop railing, lifted the radio over my head, and hurled it with all my strength. Out and down it sailed.

The Philco landed on a patch of barren ground, one corner driven first on a smooth flat rock. The wood case shattered and splintered, the beige grill cloth crumpled. Glass shards erupted in a spray of burst tubes and dial fragments catching the morning sun.

My ears had been ringing with panic and exertion. Slowly it began to subside, and the morning sounds returned. Birds, the whir of cicadas. Aside from that and a car going down the road, all was still. Could it be over? There was only one way to find out, to look. I walked down the stairs and slowly approached the destroyed radio. A yellowish ichor, thin pus streaked with blood, oozed from the ruptured box. I gagged on the stench of decay and disease.

Later, I buried the mess right there in the yard.

Of Aunt-Gram's funeral that Sunday afternoon I remember little…a few distant relatives, a potluck. We told ourselves again and again that she had led a good long life, that it was a blessing she died this way instead of going ga-ga, or worse (and this in a hush), of c-a-n-c-e-r. Yes, she was lucky.

I don't know. Or, rather, I DID know. I did know that there was evil that sought *her* destruction, *our* destruction. That there were torments of the damned and maybe even the innocent. I DID know that Aunt-Gram had been lured to her death and perhaps into hell. Of the latter, there was no way for me to be certain.

> *Wisdom is better than weapons of war: but one sinner destroyeth much good.*
> —*Ecclesiastes 9:18*

Shortly after college, as both a precaution and a penance, I went high church, what low-church Anglicans call "smells and bells." I pray weekly for Aunt-Gram's soul in her own congregation's language. I figure that should do as much as anything else I can for her. I pray that in destroying the radio, I freed Aunt-Gram and destroyed the Mabel-Kaiser-thing. If virtue, love, and kindness held any power, Aunt-Gram would not suffer in the world beyond this one. But I couldn't be sure.

I pray for my own paltry soul as well.

As for the modern electronic miracles of this postmodern age, I'll have none of 'em in my house: no radio, no television, no computers. If Mrs. Kaiser found her way to me once she might well do so again.

"How odd!" people say when they come to visit. I do not make explanation.

# Abaddon

The car pulled off the main thoroughfare onto the narrow side road, crushing under its tires the thick new snow. The wind was down now, but white flakes still filled the air, illumined like confetti in the direct swath of the car's headlights.

The driver paused, rolled down his window, and studied the sign: The New Jerusalem Road. For all its promise of glory, there was no sign of recent travel; the fresh snow was unbroken by tire tracks, a smooth white corridor between the darkness on either side. Coming off the paved and plowed main road, the car fishtailed as it again started forward.

The driver had memorized the directions only that afternoon for the route he must follow; he wanted to be able to keep his eyes on the road. The only time he shifted his study was to query the odometer. There were four miles left to him on this trip. Four miles until he could ask for a very specific favor.

At exactly the four-mile mark, he paused again at a drive, also unplowed. A stone arch demarked it. He turned in, shifted into first gear, and crept forward. Stone walls running beside the drive fell behind as he approached the house; it was perhaps a quarter mile in all. Only a dim porch light shone through the snow. Nowhere else was there any sign of life. But he knew he was expected.

At last, the car was before the main house, three stories, the first of dressed stone and timbered above, surmounted by a steep-pitched roof. Dormers looked blankly into the night. Dimly, he could make out some peripheral buildings—one of them a barn—far back by a tree line. At the tree line, a large, wooded hill vanished into the night and snow. The visitor carefully collected his briefcase and his hat, counted and climbed the seven stairs to the entryway, and signaled his presence using a large cast-iron knocker. He stood, shifting from one booted foot to the other. At no time did he take his eyes from the door. Nor was there anything unexpected to see even had he turned around to gaze over the wide field that separated the house from the road. There was only wild country for miles and miles about, disused fields, woods, wetlands with cattails standing above the frozen surface.

In the cold stillness the visitor heard the approach of feet ringing on stone flooring, the rattle of the door handle, and he saw the movement of the door within its frame. He stood facing a young man, perhaps in his late twenties.

"We're relieved that you've arrived safely," said the young man, opening the massive door wide. "These early winter snows are unpredictable." The guest unzipped and removed his boots, unwrapped his scarf, and shucked himself out of his heavy wool coat. He handed everything but the briefcase to the young man, who disappeared with them through a nearby doorway.

At his return, unencumbered, he motioned for the visitor to follow. "Mr. Abaddon is in his study and will receive you there."

The visitor, still firmly clutching his briefcase, followed in silence as they moved to what he thought would be the back of the house. But no. One corridor led to another and thence from wing to wing, each successively older. Plaster walls gave way to timber, which in turn gave way to naked stone, dressed, and fit with obvious skill and care.

At last, they paused at an oak-paneled door. Both the door and its frame were slightly askew, the left side higher than the right. When opened, though, its hinges betrayed no grating or other sound of tension. The visitor walked into the room as his guide held the door. On the far side of the room close to a fireplace was a massive desk with a man seated behind it. Here sat Mr. Abaddon, master of the house. He was writing and displayed no reaction to the visitor's intrusion upon his privacy until he finished, signed the page, and set it aside.

He raised his grizzled head and studied his guest, much as his guest studied him. In the lamp light and the light from the fire, the guest saw a large man, powerfully built, and attired in a suit from an earlier era. His close-cropped grey hair, his large but sharply angled head combined with hooded eyes gave him the appearance of a snake, a dangerous snake. His widely set eyes, seemingly obsidian, glittered. At last, he addressed the man standing before him: "Mr. Dunlevy, you would ask a favor of me? Come, then, sit down and let us talk." He indicated a chair. Dunlevy lowered himself into the upholstered seat. If it weren't for the fact of two small windows in the exterior stone wall, he could have imagined himself far underground. The night pressed against them.

The visitor—Dunlevy—was neither a large nor small man; he was strangely nondescript. His hair, his eyes, his suit, and his shoes ... all were brown. There appeared very little he could summon in the way of reserve—he looked played out, exhausted—and when the guide offered him a drink, he accepted it with soft thanks.

His host began: "What, Mr. Dunlevy, do you know of Geoffrey Abaddon? And more to the point, what would draw you out on such a night?"

Dunlevy took a drink from his glass before answering. His voice was soft but insistent.

"I know that you and your people have been here—in this house...or parts of it—since this state was first settled. I know you own about half the county under one name or another. And I know you and your family have a reputation of sometimes being able to help people who have special... problems." Dunlevy leaned forward. "I have a very special problem."

"Surely, you're not wanted by the authorities," said Mr. Abaddon, smiling slightly. He paused and took in a large breath. "No...I would guess it might have more to do with the death of your wife." Dunlevy's head jerked up. Abaddon nodded in the direction of the guide and continued: "My assistant, Mr. Neville, was able to complete some preliminary researches after you set up our appointment."

Dunlevy took another pull at his drink and nodded. "As a matter of fact, it does deal with my late wife. There's something wrong, terribly wrong, and I want it put right...if that's even possible."

"Go on," said Abaddon, nodding.

"If you know my wife died, perhaps you know that she died a terribly painful death. The cancer ate at her. After her first surgery the doctors told us that she didn't stand much chance. We wouldn't take their word for it and searched desperately for other options. I spent hours, days, in medical libraries. All the literature confirmed the diagnosis, but we still had hope of a miracle. The entire time she fought as best she could. When the pain was bad there were drugs, but she so wanted to stay awake, to stay alert, that she fought them, too. She rarely complained.

"Her death—when it came this last summer—wasn't a surprise or even that much of a shock. She had suffered so that I felt a very strong sense of relief for her.

"I miss her terribly. We were not only man and wife, but she was truly my very best friend. Not a minute goes by without some thought of her; I catch myself making mental notes to share with her when I see her next. And then, of course, I realize that I won't.

"She was something of a poet, at least I thought she was, and she also kept a journal. While she was alive, I judged those items private. But last month—it was my birthday and about four months since she died—I needed a sense of her, so I collected a sheaf of her poems; they were all in a file drawer. And I started reading them.

"They were love poems. But they weren't to me or even about me. How did I know? She described the man as very fair, blond, thin to the point of emaciation, tall, long limbed. As you can see, I am none of those things. I puzzled over the poems for hours. I was more stunned than anything. And finally, in one of her journals I found the entry that gave this man a name. That same poem explained the power he held over my wife: he had raped her. I knew from my wife that she had been assaulted several years before we met; she told me some but not all the facts. I assumed that she had put that behind her.

"Mr. Abaddon, this man is in everything she wrote!"

The young assistant came forward with a fresh drink; Dunlevy took it eagerly as he resumed.

"For days I couldn't do anything. I never left home. Then, the more I thought the more I came to realize that my wife—no matter what she wrote—was not physically unfaithful to me. I am as sure of that as anything I know. But for all our marriage, some 19 years, this man has been a part of our marriage—and I DIDN'T KNOW IT."

Dunlevy slumped into his chair. Mr. Abaddon leaned forward, hunching over the desk.

"Your anger is understandable, but may you not be mistaken? Could the poems after all be about you, or perhaps some imaginary lover? What makes you so certain?"

Dunlevy shifted in his chair.

"As I said, she finally named him in her journal. She wrote about her attraction; she called it 'limerence.' And

I've met this man," he said. "I knew he was a former serious boyfriend, and I was never thrilled to have him about when we were dating. But he came to our wedding, and he occasionally wrote to my wife. Once, he even came to see her. And she told me she had dinner with him as well—once—when she travelled to Chicago on business. Chicago! That's where he lives and works.

"He even came to her funeral. Had I known then what I know now, I probably would have…." He closed his eyes, and swallowed. Then he resumed: "After the funeral he had the nerve to sit in my house and talk about our 'mutual' loss.

"He, Mr. Abaddon, is the blue-eyed blond, he is the one with whom she once was in love. He was rich and privileged, and she had worshipped him, perhaps as an ideal. And he raped her more than twenty-two years ago. He forced her when she'd had too much to drink; she knew what was happening, but she was unable to stop it. And all these years that ate away, threatened her sense of control. There's no way I could ever prove it, but I think it caused her cancer.

"And I feel powerless. What can I do? Go to Chicago and hunt him down?"

Dunlevy appeared an unlikely agent of vengeance. He stopped and looked beseechingly at his host.

"And that brings me for my reasons to be here. I've heard that sometimes you… manage things of this nature. Perhaps you'll be able to give me more information. If that's all, it will be enough."

Mr. Abaddon had settled back in his chair and sat studying his steepled fingers. "Will it?"

Dunlevy did not answer.

"Well, Mr. Dunlevy, as you say, sometimes things are accomplished. First, I will investigate. At the risk of intrusion, may I please read these poems?"

Dunlevy picked up the briefcase he'd placed by the side of his chair, snapped the latches, and pulled out a stack of papers. Dunlevy slid the manuscript across the desk. "I've made photocopies and brought them. Please promise you'll destroy them when you've finished?"

Mr. Abaddon nodded as he reached to accept the poems. "I'm more likely to return them. And, of course, I'll need this man's name."

"Franke, David Franke. He does some sort of work for a large charitable foundation. He's married and has two daughters. I don't want to hurt them. As far as I'm concerned, they're innocent. I wouldn't think his wife would know any of this."

"Mr. Dunlevy, surely you must understand that our affair is likely to have a sum zero outcome," said Mr. Abaddon. His eyes shone in the lamp light. "I mean, Mr. Dunlevy, that if we win, he loses. Of course, your sense is that HE has won, and YOU have lost. But it may not be that simple. Your wife had a role that she played in all of this. Why did she stay infatuated with this man, with this KIND of man?"

"I don't know," said Dunlevy. "I've read of other cases since I discovered her journals. It could be like a Stockholm syndrome. It happens in some rape cases. And the results...."

"Can you imagine forgiving this man?" Abaddon asked bluntly. "Do you...pray?"

Dunlevy shook his head. "I've tried prayer. I want justice."

"Justice may not be to your liking," said Mr. Abaddon. "Are you certain about this course of action?"

Dunlevy nodded.

"Very well, we begin."

"Your fee?"

"... Has already been collected," said Mr. Abaddon. "Mr. Neville will see you out."

The thin young man was at Dunlevy's elbow. As the two walked from the room Dunlevy stole one more glance into the study and found himself fixed in the steady gaze of its occupant. There may have been pity in that look.

As he was fitting the guest into his coat, Mr. Neville told Dunlevy what to expect. "You may not hear from me for weeks, perhaps months. Don't call. You need only know that Mr. Abaddon is working on the matter, and I'll contact you when we have something to report."

Dunlevy adjusted his coat against the cold as he approached his car. He climbed in and keyed the engine. The circle drive led him again to the road and he disappeared the way he came, pushing snow all the while.

January froze into February, and February into March. The state recorded the highest snowfall in a decade. Forecasters and old-timers recalled the winter of 1936 as analogous.

Late March saw Dunlevy again head out to The New Jerusalem Road. He had been summoned by Mr. Neville. There was news and Mr. Abaddon wished to convey it in person.

Instead of fresh fallen snow, there was slush and mud. His car slid among rutted tracks. Water filled his tire impressions; fractured shards of ice floated in them when he passed. The sunset filled the sky with red. Though yet far off, spring would come.

This time he was able to see the estate more clearly as he turned off the road and onto the property. The wet stone lower wall of the house added to a sense of inevitable destruction by the slow turn of nature.

He was met at the door by Mr. Neville.

"Thank you for your call. I've been waiting, but, quite frankly, I was beginning to doubt...."

As before, Mr. Neville took his hat, coat, and boots and led the way through the ages of the house to the study. This time Abaddon kept his eyes on Dunlevy as he entered the room and seated himself in the chair of his last visit. The two men sat in silence for perhaps sixty seconds. Finally, Dunlevy cleared his throat.

"Yes, I have much to report," said Mr. Abaddon. "But first you need to know something of how I work. You were right when you suggested that my family has been here a long, long time. We have established a reputation and a series of contacts throughout this part of the country. We are known even in the financial capitols of the world. I am the only one who makes this estate my home, Mr. Dunlevy; I am the only one of this generation called to remain here. But there are my brothers and sisters, many cousins—in short, a whole network of trustworthy confederates. It is to them that I turn when I must know more. It is they who have aided us."

Abaddon stopped and fixed his gaze on Dunlevy. He smiled slightly. "Franke is dead," he announced.

Dunlevy sat upright.

Abaddon waved his hand dismissively. "No, we didn't kill him. He did that for himself. But in some small way we were responsible. You must judge for yourself just to what degree we are culpable…and for that matter to what degree you, yourself, must stand the blame." At Dunlevy's perplexed expression, Abaddon continued: "My first thought was that your wife may have written about an imaginary tryst, or perhaps ascribed all her desires to this man for lack of a better focus. Then, after reading the file, I came to agree with you.

"I began investigating to find other instances of rape perpetrated by Mr. Franke. Yes, Mr. Dunlevy, there were others; a rapist is rarely content with just one assault. Curiously, never had charges been filed. Proof—legal proof—would be nearly impossible after so long a time in the cases we found. And the statute of limitations has long passed. So, it fell to us to undertake other avenues.

"And we found them. Mr. Franke, consistent in his personality, assumed that he could get away with anything—including siphoning off funds from his employers. In one case, he was let go without charges to avoid a scandal. In his most recent job, our investigation revealed that he had taken very nearly nine-hundred thousand dollars.

"Once we had the evidence, our investigator felt it incumbent to share the information with the authorities; by chance that investigator was a member of the board of trustees of the organization that employed Franke. The results were a quick investigation and confirmation from the foundation office, Franke's arrest, and arraignment. He was bound over for trial but had been released on bail. His suicide was a preliminary balancing of the books. He was home with his family, went upstairs to his bedroom and shot himself in the head. He wanted to be very certain of the outcome."

Mr. Abaddon held out a newspaper clipping which confirmed all the details. Dunlevy scanned the piece. "Surely, it was just a matter of time before he was caught?"

"Perhaps. Perhaps not. The better question might be: Has justice been served? What do you think?"

Dunlevy paused to rub his chin. "Well, I feel it has."

"Do you? And what of his wife? What of his children, even though they are young adults? Will they see this as justice, too?"

"I'm sorry for them. I know this is going to hurt them all the rest of their lives, but Franke should have thought of that long ago. He was not an innocent man. He deserved to die."

"We all die, Mr. Dunlevy. We all deserve to die. The question I'm asking is this: Are YOU satisfied?"

Dunlevy sat absorbed in his thoughts for several minutes. Outside the last of the twilight glowed through the windowpanes, a grandfather clock across the room softly chimed the hour.

"No, I guess not."

Again, they sat in silence. At last Dunlevy shifted and spoke.

"... Well, let's say that I thought I'd feel a lot better about having him pay some kind of price."

"Do you think he's paid that price? Has he suffered enough to bring justice to your wife's soul?"

"You know, Mr. Abaddon, it feels like we're comparing apples and oranges. One does not equal the other."

Dunlevy slumped against the cushions.

"Yours is an observation I would classify as coming from Sophia, the goddess of wisdom. There can be no equal measures of justice. Beyond that, Mr. Dunlevy, the more this is with you, the more it will weigh against your conscience. Do you remember my question during your earlier visit of whether you were given to prayer?"

Dunlevy nodded.

"I commend that course to you now."

Mr. Abaddon's eyes glinted and sparkled. "I am sorry for you, Mr. Dunlevy. You were right when you surmised that someone else was a partner to your marriage, a silent but most deadly partner. Please accept my condolences." He took out a thick envelope from his center desk drawer. "Oh, here are the copies of your wife's poems and journal entries. I am satisfied we were able to bring this matter to an end."

Dunlevy took the envelope and turned to leave the room. Mr. Neville had opened the door as the conversation ended and now escorted his guest.

They walked in silence through the great house, from the ancient to the more contemporary construction. In the entryway Mr. Neville handed Dunlevy his boots. The guest sat in a waiting chair to put them on and then stood and was helped into his coat. At last, he was handed his hat and ushered through the door.

Dunlevy stood on the step, straining against the new night. He turned to the young man. "I don't suppose most of your cases are along these lines?"

The young man shrugged: "I could not tell you even if I wanted to. I assure you, Mr. Dunlevy, we are discreet. I bid you good night, and if ever you need our help again, please don't hesitate to ask."

Dunlevy shuddered visibly, assented, and slowly walked down the steps to his car.

There was something missing, he knew, from his understanding. As he keyed the engine and engaged the transmission, he could foresee a long period of muddled thinking and confused recollection. It was as though he'd had the experience but missed its meaning.

But there would be no return to Geoffrey Abaddon.

## Through a Glass, Darkly

The funeral wasn't 'til eleven, but I arrived early, a little after ten, and found no one at the door to greet me. I could find my own way in the mortuary. The correct room was clearly marked with a noticeboard beside the doorframe: Mr. Arthur Roberts.

The entry was at the back of the room. At the front, carefully lit and made up, lay Art, my remote cousin. I made my way to him. The mortician had done a good job, but then, he'd had good material to start with. Art was a handsome man . . . big and with rugged good looks. In death he looked . . . well, I suppose, dead. But noble. He had fought a good fight against the cancer that consumed him at age 71. In fact, he'd returned from a trip to Spain only two weeks before he died. It was on the trip back that he had begun feeling seriously ill; before then, his terminal disease had been merely an inconvenience.

His face was, naturally enough, thinner than I remembered, but there was the clear remainder of the aquiline nose, the patrician brow. He looked like a man who could sing—which he did, frequently and well. He knew all the show tunes, the movie tunes, and popular tunes. Art had been an accomplished socialite and, though he had remained a bachelor, had formed true and lasting friendships with both men and women.

Looking down at him I knew with certainty that I was going to miss him. He had guided so much of my life with his good humor and wit. And now it had come to this. Even in life we are in death, says St. Paul.

My reverie was snapped by bustle at the back of the room. I turned to see Cousin Ruthanne coming toward me. Actually, she's Cousin Walter's wife, but she and Art and Walter had made a lifetime of being friends and family, no small accomplishment. And it had fallen to her to guide Cousin Art to that door of death. Though she lived 35 miles from him, she had come whenever he called, to take him to doctors, lawyers, real estate agents . . . wherever there were needful duties to be done. And, bless her, she had held his hand as he died.

Ruthanne had the strength to be cheerful under almost any circumstance. I have seen her smile through her own tears on many occasions. She says we have an obligation to try to be happy no matter what happens to us. Art was now out of pain, and for her that was enough cause for rejoicing.

"Oh, Scotty, I'm so glad you could come. When I called you, I knew that you might not be able to make it, and that would have been all right. After all, you had to come clear across the state, and on a workday, too."

I assured her that I would have come under any circumstance. She was gratified and stood with me at the casket.

"I think he looks really good from this angle . . . just like he used to. But if you stand over there," she said, pointing to Art's feet, "then he looks like somebody else.

"The kids aren't here yet," she said of her two offspring, Gloria and Richard. "Dick's supposed to give the eulogy, and I want to make sure that he invites two of Art's bridge buddies to say a few words.

"And the priest isn't here, yet, either. We had to get a substitute for Father Alcane at St. Anselm's; he's gone for two weeks. It turns out his old teacher, Father Borley, is staying at the rectory. He's long retired, but he's going to do the service. The church secretary said she'll make sure he's here on time. She's going to drive him over and drop him off . . . he's too old to drive himself."

Ruthanne explained that the service would be short; Art wasn't a church member and didn't take too much to liturgy. The priest was to give a short homily. Certainly, he wouldn't go into the burial office because Art wasn't going to be buried right away. He was slated for cremation after the service with interment at some later date.

When people started arriving, Ruthanne left me to go stand by the door. Almost all went to pay their last respects and see if they could find the flower arrangements they'd sent. Art loved flowers, but I hadn't sent any. I figured it would be just one more task for Ruthanne after the service.

I had to admit that Art had some pretty classy looking friends. Even the women who were in their seventies and eighties were turned out in fashion, some revealingly so. Art would have loved it and made some witty and mildly naughty comment. I just looked.

As the clock swung past quarter-to, Ruthanne was plainly fidgeting. I went to stand by her to learn that neither Dick nor the old priest had arrived. One of them, I knew, would hear about it later. I excused myself to use the restroom and on the way back saw Dick being shepherded into an office. Ruthanne was at his elbow. Behind them wandered a vague and seemingly dazed older person. This had to be the priest; the cassock was a dead giveaway. He shuffled in after Dick and Ruthanne. I headed back to my seat with some misgivings of what was to come. At the very worst it would all be over in an hour.

Everyone had been seated; a few fidgeted. The funeral director, a moderately young man who had introduced himself to me as Roger Smithson, closed the main entry door. Within a minute he was opening a smaller door at the front of the room. In shuffled the relic that I took for Fr. Borley.

He stood before the casket, looking down at Cousin Art. I gave a start when he first spoke; his voice was so strong, rich and deep, much more full than I'd ever expect from his dry old husk. And he spoke with a cultivated British accent.

"'I am the resurrection and the life,' saith our Lord. 'He that believeth in me, though he be dead, yet shall he live.'"

Then he turned and looked over all of us who were his audience.

"Why are we here?" He looked around the room again, filling his eyes with the lot of us. He smiled as though we were the dearest sight for his old eyes.

"Certainly this is a very sad occasion for those of you who knew Arthur Roberts. From the size of this gathering, I'd have to assume that he was known by many people . . . and loved by many people. Funerals—especially in this day and age—are not obligatory. We attend one such as this as a matter of respect, affection, and sometimes, love.

"That, then, is why we are here . . . as a measure of our feeling for this man who has died. It is a sad day for you, but I am convinced that it is not a sad day for Arthur. In fact, I know that it was a joyous day for him as soon as he died to this world. At that very instant he was born anew to another world, the next world, the waiting and coming world of our Lord Jesus Christ.

"Now, I say this with some assurance. These are not claims I make lightly or on my own authority.

"Consider this from the Old Testament . . . the 23rd Psalm...."

He recited the song, carrying it on his regular breathing, the susurration of our soft voices accompanying him. At its conclusion he resumed his deliberation.

"Imagine being in the company of God for as long as you want, having access to the Great Answerer of Job, the loving presence who would not want you to suffer in unknowingness. I know you have heard that 23rd Psalm more times than you'd care to remember, most often at funerals; we all have. But its application is far more broad. First of all, what if it were true? ...That goodness and mercy would follow you wherever you go, whenever you went?"

He shifted on his feet, and his cassock swayed about his thinness. He smiled brightly, his face aglow. His eyes flashed and the skin around them crinkled with an inner smile. I could not help but smile back, as did others. There was something here beyond the scripture.

"I used to wonder how that could be true, but I am convinced beyond all reckoning.

"St. Paul, in his letter to the Romans put it this way:

"'For I am persuaded, that neither death, nor life, nor angels, nor principalities, nor powers, nor things present, nor things to come,

"Nor height, nor depth, nor any other creature, shall be able to separate us from the love of God, which is in Christ Jesus our Lord.'"

Again Fr. Borley looked about the room. As his eyes went over my face, I saw that he was filled with wonder. I reflected that such faith must be a real gift. How else could one who was surely contemplating his own mortality speak with such assurance? Was he 90? Even older? The years didn't matter, though: there was in him a compelling attraction that invited my attention and belief.

"And beyond this," he said, beginning with renewed vigor, "Our Lord Himself has promised us that we would be with him and he with us. Even as He hung on the cross, our Savior promised the penitent thief that 'This day thou shalt be with me in Paradise.' By that we know we shall be with him when we die. We do not go into oblivion, and—God sparing us—we shall not go to Hell.

"But our Savior also told us that he would be among us: 'Lo, I am with you to the end of the world.' He will be here, and if we will be with him, then when we die, we shall be here as well.

"That means that Arthur is with us today. Right here and right now. We cannot see him, but perhaps we can sense him. He has left the body and is now part of the larger eternity . . . at all places at all times."

Fr. Borley looked into my eyes yet again and seemed to linger before his gaze moved on.

"This, my very dear friends, is the promise that Christ made to us. I ask you to believe it, for it is true beyond the shadow of a doubt.

"And now let us pray—as we have been taught—the Lord's Prayer...."

We were no longer quietly accompanying him. We had been emboldened, and voices—high and low—joined until we were much louder than Fr. Borley "...For ever and ever. Amen."

We had surprised ourselves, I'm guessing. There was a general shuffling and some mild throat clearing. With a warmly knowing smile, Fr. Borley picked up the narrative thread.

"Arthur's young cousin, Richard, will begin by offering some remembrances now."

Fr. Borley nodded to Cousin Richard who rose to assume the role. With a lingering look around the room, Fr. Borley stepped out into the hall, where I assumed he was observing the memorial.

Richard did a splendid job. And he was the first among several. Art's friends and family recounted many telling stories of his life, his generosity of spirit. He also had a world class ability to exasperate, most often because he was invariably late for appointments and meetings. ...Late but apologetic. Always it was his fault; he never evaded responsibility. In other areas of his life, though, whenever anything had happened to him, Art put together a first-class story, if not an altogether true one. He was often the butt of these telling vignettes. Almost all of us had heard tales about his light romances, his frequent travel, his bridge encounters, and his life spent pursuing the fine arts. We recalled many events that served to remind us of Art.

Dick kept the comments from Art's friends rolling along at a good clip. Mostly we laughed together. There were times when one or two had to stop to make way for their tears, but we waited; there was no embarrassment.

I was wiping a few tears of my own when I saw Fr. Borley move close to the door, waiting to re-enter the room, a peaceful smile upon his face, his eyes glittering with what I thought was amusement.

Just then I heard the phone ring once in the office. Mr. Smithson left the room, passing by the priest. Fr. Borley watched him go. And then the old man noted my eye on him. His smile broadened, he tilted his head to the right and stepped back from the door, so he was out of my view.

Dick finished up the comments of the others with a wonderful story about accidently on-purpose locking Art out of the room when they were traveling in Europe. Dick was 13 at the time. Art's revenge was simply to order snails for Dick—in French—the next day at lunch. Dick had half the order down before he said that it didn't taste like shrimp.

And, laughing, Dick said Fr. Borley would close with a final prayer. Dick bowed his head and waited. One by one we looked toward the door, expecting the old man to rejoin us. I, for one, was looking forward to the sound of his voice. But he was not again among us. We were treated to silence, then light conversation as Dick shrugged his shoulders and walked out to the hall to see if Fr. Borley might be in the bathroom. He returned scratching his head.

"Uh, Fr. Borley seems to have wandered away. I'm sure he'll be right back, but let me offer the prayer."

At the conclusion, Dick invited us to file past the casket for one more look. In my turn I held back my tears and looked over at Cousin Ruthanne for strength. She, in turn, was sitting between the undertaker, Mr. Smithson, and someone whom I'd never seen, a mild little woman not quite dressed for the funeral. Ruthanne was very slowly shaking her head back and forth.

I wandered over to hear Ruthanne saying, "But he was here. Right here. No more than 15 minutes ago."

I stood by until Ruthanne looked up at me and explained.

"This is Verna . . . Robles?"

The little woman nodded her close-cropped greying head.

"She's the secretary at St. Anselm's. She was supposed to drive Fr. Borley here, but when she went to get him, she found him slumped over the rectory desk. She says he's dead and has been since at least ten thirty."

Ruthanne looked up confused. She reached for Verna's delicate hand.

"She didn't call here until we were almost through the ceremony," Ruthanne continued. "And then she couldn't believe what Mr. Smithson told her. She had to come over . . . just as soon as the doctor certified him dead. He's now stretched out on the floor in the rectory with one of the nuns watching over him. She hasn't even called the undertaker. Of course, she's here now and can just tell Mr. Smithson . . ."

Cousin Ruthanne began to laugh. The circumstances were so singular that I had to join in.

Poor Mrs. Robles was sorely disconcerted by our evident humor. She plucked a tissue from the box on a nearby table and glared at us in turn.

Barely controlling myself, I also reached for a tissue to wipe away my tears. "I'm sorry," I said. "It's just that Fr. Borley was here. All of us saw and heard him. And you say he's dead? You must pardon us if we find it hard to believe. Perhaps we had a different Fr. Borley here? About late 80s or past 90? Maybe five-seven or -eight? Intricately worked surplice, maybe with a tatted border?"

"Yes, tatted," said Mrs. Robles. "But his voice was weak, very weak, and he couldn't have looked at you. Fr. Borley was blind and has been these 20 years."

At the risk of seeming an absolute lunatic, I begged Mrs. Robles to bring us a photograph of Fr. Borley. There had to be one somewhere. She looked up at me with displeasure. She had done enough, it was clear. So, I asked if I might accompany her on her return trip and either look at the photograph myself or—better yet—see for myself the remains of the good Father.

She looked from me to Mr. Smithson and finally nodded. But she was frowning. "Suit yourself," she said.

We left in a rush, and I told Cousin Ruthanne that I'd catch up with her at the funeral luncheon.

I drove my own car, following Mrs. Robles. With some measure of hesitancy she allowed me in the door of the massive old rectory. Then she led the way through the dining room and to the closed door of the study; she paused before opening it.

On the floor, dressed in his full liturgical robes, lay the body of a shriveled old man. Even in death there was no question: here was Fr. Borley. And unlikely as it might seem, even in death I could detect a trace of a smile remaining on his face.

I nodded and knelt to pray beside his remains, a move that quite surprised the good woman standing beside me.

I rose at the conclusion of my private prayer of thanksgiving and left with these perhaps audible words: "He knew whereof he spoke."

## Fat of the Land

Issue IV, Vol. 24, *Modern Dietary Practices*

From the Editor—

Dear Readers:

You are accustomed to the odd cases I bring for your consideration from time to time. What follows has been sent on to me by Dr. Edwin Lassiter of Edenton, which is a small city in northwestern Ohio. I have known Dr. Lassiter for twenty years (more or less). We are colleagues and have served together on various institutional boards. No one who knows him could describe him as fanciful or given to whimsy; he is first and foremost a scientist. I have never before had cause to doubt his reason. I do not doubt him now; but I will admit that this account of his patient stretches my sense of the believable. I pass along this account, two drawings, and his request for reports of any other similarities in other cases within the dietary community.

Stanley Yates, Editor

> *Dear Stanley:*
>
> *I wonder if I might impose upon our friendship to ask you to look over this manuscript from one of*

*my patients. I must confess that I am at a loss. And Hugo is verily and truly missing. He was being treated—if we can call it that—by me for his obesity. He is one of those most unfortunate people for whom diet and exercise do nothing. And after careful consideration, he refused bariatric surgery; he is correct in his observation that the risks are NOT inconsequential. I was working with him on acceptance—for there really was little else I had to offer in such a case, except my friendship. I liked Hugo. He was intelligent, well read, somewhat wary and cynical. He also had a gift that might have given him some relief from the stares and unwelcome comments. He was a talented artist in pencil. I have a portrait that he made of me from memory. It shows me in study at my desk. At first, I thought it a rather inexact rendering, but when I asked about how he did it, he described a process called blind contour: the artist does not look at the paper, does not lift the pencil from the paper, and attempts to draw what he or she sees. Or, in this case remembers. I suspect Hugo had a highly developed visual memory, the eidetic memory, if you will. Then, as I studied it, I grew amazed; it was a combination of what he saw in recall and the way I saw myself. I told him how much I appreciated his gift. It hangs in my home.*

*I had urged him to make use of that art to claim his rightful place as a contributing member of society. But no. That was not the way for him. I gather he had other gifts, too. My medical assistant observed that he was very humorous. (As you know I am not much given to laughter and joking.) I think Hugo saw his position most clearly and would have said he was coming to terms with his lot until all this happened. What follows is a journal of some pretty improbable rambling. Still,*

*as Sherlock Holmes asked of Watson: "How often have I said to you that when you have eliminated the impossible, whatever remains, however improbable, must be the truth?" (I HAD read Arthur Conan Doyle in my youth.)*

*Hugo was reported missing on the date following his last entry. He didn't show up for work and his supervisor sent someone out, sure he was going to find a case of infarct, dead in bed. After all, Hugo had called in sick the day before. The searchers were surprised when only this missive was found. Hugo's car was in the driveway and the neighbors hadn't seen him leaving the premises; some of them are fairly observant, not to say nosy. His backyard neighbor, Mrs. Murdoch, says she saw him sunning himself that day—even though it was overcast—stretched out on a lawn chair. When she checked five minutes later, he was gone, but he'd left behind an iced tea with ice still in the glass. Oh, and his clothes, as though he'd been removed from them. They remained on the chaise lounge. Mrs. Murdoch says she was scandalized by the idea of a large, naked man wandering the neighborhood.*

*That was it. Since then, there have been no sightings. He didn't leave town by bus, and no one has seen him in the downtown.*

*I'm stumped. What do you think? What do your readers think? Are there other doctors who are losing patients in a like fashion? Obese ones? I'm not being facetious, and for that reason I ask you to ask them.*

*NB: The title and the typescript are mine. Hugo had carefully entered his observations in a handwritten journal. I transcribed, correcting very small matters of spelling and punctuation. For the most part his compositional skills were flawless.*

*There must be a logical explanation, but just now it eludes me. I have a few closing comments that you'll note at the end.*

*Cordially,*

*Ed (Dr. Edwin Lassiter)*

## THE JOURNAL OF HUGO MORRISON, LATE OF THIS PLANET

### WEDNESDAY, June 17

I had been daydreaming again. My pen and notebook slipped from between my fingers and had fallen to the grass beneath me. Already carefully stretched out on a heavy-duty lawn lounger, I eased my bulk to the side to reach the pen and notebook. I grunted with the effort, stretching out my fingers. At last I felt the pen, then the notebook and, rejoicing, reclaimed them to my breast. In celebration I raised my legs to hoist my feet into view, an activity normally precluded by my more than ample girth. My toes waved at me from places I can no longer reach without undue strain.

Oh, I have grown fat, almost gloriously fat, were it anything in which to glory. Instead, people who would never talk with a stranger about a missing leg or having two heads make free to tell me that I'm obese—as if I hadn't a clue—or that I'm going to die soon from overworking my heart, another comforting thought.

They must imagine that because I'm so fat I'm also well insulated against their cruel barbs. Would they like it if I told them their children were ugly or stupid? Or, that they dressed without imagination or style? Or, that they would likely pass on their same insensitivity to their children and grandchildren?

They say they tell me that I'm fat for my own good. They're so concerned that they shout their comments from moving cars or across a parking lot or even a field in the park. Rude, rude, rude. Really, it's more of some inner need they have to be able to impose their standards on me. I do wish I could oblige them. Could I be rake thin I would be so in an instant, simply to get these nincompoops off my backside.

I have had nearly a lifetime of such observations. I had been a normal boy, the child and sibling of normally weighted people. When I hit puberty, something went awry. I grew taller, of course, but I grew fatter with each passing day.

As a student, even my very name was turned against me. I had been named for a great uncle who in turn had been named to honor the French writer, Victor Hugo. My fellow students very quickly changed that to Huge-O. And it has stuck. Just last month I ran into one of my classmates, and the horrid moniker sailed from between his teeth. I would have liked to have handed those teeth to him in a box.

My parents took me at first to our local doctor. He ran all the tests, and everything came back well in the normal range; nothing excessive, except my weight. Other specialists found nothing more, but in the process, I was liberally poked, prodded, desanguinated (not to say ex-), measured, measured, measured. My loving but alarmed parents were mortified at my increasing girth. I was mortified by it, too, but what could I do? I still had to eat; my body commands it.

It's far more than a matter of will. I have starved myself repeatedly. I can do that. Every diet only leads me further and further into frustration. Once my caloric intake is trimmed my body gets by on almost nothing. I can eat only fibrous foods and still gain weight. And the initial starvation eventually would result in a binge. ...Well, a binge for me, but probably not for a normal person. At the end of each dieting session, I would weigh substantially more than when I started. I have given up on that.

I have come to accept that there is no hope. I am unwilling to undergo bariatric surgery. Dr. Lassiter agreed there are risks, risks I am unwilling to take. So, I am left with no hope. Dr. Lassiter has been as much help as he can be, but there's little anyone has to offer me. I am going through life as a fat man, a great big fat man. A gargantuan fat man. (After Rabelais' 16th Century character Gargantua; I DO read. A lot.) My gratitude to the universe extends to this: I am not nor am I likely to become the world's heaviest man. Neither have I joined the ranks of the 600-pounders, so minutely chronicled on reality television. Instead, I balance these days at about four hundred fifty pounds, a mighty and uncomfortable bulk. And expensive: I require special order shirts, pants, shoes, even underwear...all designed to make the most of me.

But as I lay there on and sinking into the yard chair, surrounded by my too, too abundant flesh, I pondered if there might not be another way, something I've never even heard of. This thought brought about in me a longing—a nostalgia, really—as if I had lost something. And perhaps I had.

I closed my eyes and willed myself to dream of what has not been but that I felt should have been.

I am fairly certain I did not fall asleep. Instead, black flashes turned into swirls and thence into a grey, moving mist. At length I determined that it was I who was moving and not the mist. And below me, flowing like a scene unrolled in a cinema production, were fields, houses, rivers, cities. This place below me was a land, very fair, like our own but different. The colors were more intense. I flew above the landscape...whether in the body or out I could not say, heaven knows. I saw movement on the roads and paths. There were people down there—at least, they resembled people—with strange things thrown over their shoulders. By the very action of my will alone, I drifted down to them, and stood among them. I noted that I was unclothed, but I believed—I somehow knew—I was invisible.

They were thin, uniformly thin, very lightly muscled, with tan skins and dark hair. They were clothed and from the back of almost each creature there arose a...fin? No, more like a tube, some longer or shorter, and each sheathed in varying degrees of opulence. Almost all of them sported shimmering cloth, finely worked and fitted.

What I assessed as a male creature had just walked by...well, actually walked through me. I shuddered, expecting to feel the grue of the uncanny. Instead, there was nothing, not even a tingle. As he disappeared through me, I noted the tube was perhaps five inches in diameter where it joined his back and over its length of two to three feet tapered to a gentle point. I shuddered again.

I could stand it no longer. I opened my eyes and was again surrounded by my own back yard, safe in its muted colors. Had I been asleep? Or should I put the vision down to mad imaginings? To be both fat and crazy! Nonetheless, I have noted these observations.

## THURSDAY, June 18

All night at work I thought about what I had seen. I work as a security guard, one of the few industries that can make use of a fat man. Even with two college degrees, I have been unable to find a job in my field: management economics. Companies for the most part refuse to hire overweight people. So, instead, I sit in this little guard booth five everlasting nights a week and check in cars at the Forgemont Defense plant. I smile through my hurt at the last part of my shift as I wave through the management team day after day. I could be doing their jobs as effectively as they if only I had the chance. Why, I'd even taken the initiative to prepare studies on the operations at the plant. I had observed that the shift-change in managers left the operations understaffed at critical hours. The 8 a.m. rush was a traffic jam. They needed staggered arrivals over the period of an hour, earlier rather than later. I employed Mosconi's research on the matter to illustrate my point.

The plant manager, Conrad Somler, looked over my case study and proposal, and then turned it over to his crew without so much as a thank you. Oh, the idea was implemented. And then I was investigated as a security risk because I knew too much about the operations at the plant. They wanted to know where I'd come by the information. I explained that all I'd had to do was keep my eyes and ears open to understand the problems there. They couldn't believe that, especially coming from a fat man. (Fat men are universally assumed to be lazy, too, and the plan showed evidence of far too much thinking, and thinking is work. Axiomatically, I couldn't have thought these thoughts and therefore someone else must have. But the question was who?) They chewed on that and me for quite a while. I nearly lost my job, and as much as I hate it, I need it.

So, these days I do what little my job demands and keep my thinking to myself. Last night I thought about the strange and exotic creatures I'd seen in my vision. I sketched some of what I'd seen. I wanted to see them again. I'd have closed my eyes and tried to see them again even while I was there at my post, but that would have led someone to think I was sleeping; not a good look. Instead, I vowed to try the wishing experiment again the next day in the back yard.

## LATER THURSDAY

Which I did with success! ...Shades of John Carter of Barsoom. By the pure and efficient act of will I managed to return to the land of the spiked creatures. I managed to sit and watch them as they carried on their daily business in what I can only assume was a town square. In virtually all aspects they appear human and must inhabit an alternate universe of some sort. Their language is a pleasant mix of sounds, sometimes like plainsong and at others like melodious ululations. They also employ clicks and whistles.

I have seen them walking as individuals, couples, and extended families. Their greetings, beginning with an upraised palm issued at ten paces or so, are concluded with a kiss on the cheek and then turnabout—one at a time—for the examination of the dorsal protuberance. This latter is admired for its length, firmness and the sacking that surrounds it.

With this crowd, the longer the spike the better. Usually, the very young have only small horns which are prodded with every evidence of enthusiasm. I saw a small child once with none at all. The accompanying parent was the object of pitying glances and whispers. This parent nodded sadly and looked with some sorrow at her child. For her part, the little girl was quiet and appeared unwell, or at least very sad.

Others had small humps, especially some of the elderly and others who were obviously ill. These latter were the subject of pity, but pity from a distance.

The backside excrescence, then, had something to do with both health and social standing. Much like home.

There, too, the sick are viewed with suspicion. And there are such things as contagious diseases. At any rate, the—I 've really got to give the structure a name; from now on it's a harn—a combination of horn and handle. As well, the word resembles the sound the creatures make when they touch one another's.... At any rate, the harn is crucial to their daily lives.

After a time, I began to suspect that some of the harn were augmented. An older creature gave me the first hint. She was dressed in something approximating a gold lamé pantsuit. Her harn stood erect for a foot and then drooped at an unnatural angle. In fact, the fabric so twisted to give evidence that there was no continuous flesh. She was greeted by a younger couple, perhaps one of whom was her child. Only the upper harn, that first foot, was grasped in the greeting. The two younger individuals cast an amused glance at each other when the elder turned away from them.

A few who paraded in front of me won admiring glances for their lengthy harn. One woman's harn was so long that she carried it draped about her shoulder like a boa. Another, this time a man, carried his coiled over his forearm. He was, by my best guess, an elder statesman or a learned teacher for he was followed by a retinue of younger men. None of them had a harn of similar length, but several affected his walk and the angle of his elbow.

A thought struck me then. I had been sitting invisible and naked in their midst for hours. How many? And what of time's passing on my own planet? I felt the need to return, and with a great effort took my leave of this remarkable civilization. In the process, I squeezed my eyes shut.

When I opened them again, I found myself stretched out in my back yard, again in my clothes. There was returned to me a sense of myself. I could feel the weight being stacked upon me. In the land of the harn, I felt as if I weighed nothing, and now, I was being crushed by my own bulk. I labored to breathe but made very sure I kept at it. Eventually I felt able to raise my arm to read the dial on my wristwatch. I had been gone a full three hours. Perhaps time there and here were coincident. Well, it is time to drag—literally this time—myself to work.

## THURSDAY, June 25

It has been a week since my last entry. And in that week, I have found all I wanted to learn about the Harnii—that's what I've taken to calling the people of that land, the people of the harn. In my off hours I have been consumed with interest, walking among them, living among them...at first entirely without their knowledge. And while I do not begin to understand their language yet, I think I've mastered the basics of the harn. I acquired such knowledge by wandering until I found the equivalent of a university medical school. Charts and diagrams assure me that the harn is really nothing more than stored fat.

Instead of depositing fat around the body as we do, the Harnii stay thin with the exception of their harn...which is then treated with respect. This is a culture that worships fat. It's the thin who are pitied.

At an ice cream pavilion I noted on the board that the richness of the sundaes and splits were indicated by one, two, or three harn.

I even saw a Harnii so fat that he used a little two-wheel cart, something like a golf cart, to haul his harn. He was basking in the obvious admiration from females who were making some pretty obvious suggestions. I noted from that, the harn is probably not composed of erectile tissue. But he did strut.

If you noted that I said I have been among them almost without their knowledge, I should explain. I have taken to concentrating upon being able to feel my weight in the land of the Harnii. That concentration has evidently resulted in partial manifestation. I was concentrating so hard last Wednesday that I was able to feel myself bump into a walking Harnii. She was extremely annoyed at finding a person, naked, unlike any other she'd ever seen, suddenly in her path. But her eyes made contact with mine, and I knew then I was visible. My concentration lapsed and I rather imagine I faded from view. The Harnii kept turning around to see where I'd gone. Then she shrugged and stalked off, her firm young harn wiggling in a most appealing fashion.

Since then I have practiced and practiced and have been able to maintain appearance for an hour or better. The last time I manifested myself in the anatomy room at the university. The result—since I did it in the middle of a lecture session—was something of a sensation. The lead teacher could not refrain himself from grabbing my various rolls and bulges. He was laughing and crying all at the same time and eventually had to sit down, reeling in wonder.

I bade the poor man rise and spoke to him in good English, which he gave some indication of understanding. I gathered that I was just grand—literally and figuratively—in their eyes. I faded and reappeared for them several times and then allowed myself to be further poked, prodded, and measured.

I was treated with the utmost respect, even offering a covering, really a blanket of a sort, and at the end of the session a female Harnii came up to my side and indicated through pantomime that I was to accompany her. She made clear her name was just that: "Clear" (or something that sounded mighty close to it). My little joke. Marvel of marvels, she took me to eat, something more than a routine exercise with the Harnii. There were courses upon courses, each more resplendent and toothsome than the last. My hostess at first kept up, and then settled back to watch, obvious in her enjoyment. I cannot recall any other such meal where being full was a good thing, healing. Then, at the dessert, I could sustain my presence no longer and at last faded, leaving the blanket behind. I was exhausted and knew that I had to return to my home—my old home, this one. My last glimpse of Clear showed me a tear coursing down her cheek.

Where had our evolution gone so wrong and theirs so right? Or was it purely cultural? Could fat people be the object of admiration on my home planet? Some African cultures, I believe, think fat a very good manifestation. My own—as you so well know—does not. And I do not think I am bound for Africa.

But I am not sure I want to stay here, either. I went to work Tuesday and was greeted by fat salutations from the first four arrivals: Chubby, Tubby, Blubber, and Mound. After work I went to the grocery store. The stares and comments there reflected more of the same. They know nothing of my health or medical condition and yet they are willing—even anxious—to judge. These people must imagine that I don't know what I look like. I want to tell them that I have a mirror, that I know I'm fat. Fat, fat, fat, fat. When will they be satisfied? Never! Dr. Lassiter says I need to ignore all their words; they are not credible sources.

The next day, Wednesday—yesterday—I called in sick, another mark against my continued employment. I have found the possibility of something to look forward to, and so I indulged myself with visits to the Harnii.

With more practice I have been able to sustain my appearance in their world. In fact, I can stay without the huge concentration of will that was required to bring me there. I have had the luxury of several observations that include these:

- The Harnii employ a kind of telepathy. When I speak, they can sense my intention even if the words sound like nothing they've heard before. Clear, she who took me to lunch, is particularly adept at reading my heart.

- Time in both worlds runs forward at an apparently constant rate. An hour on earth is about the same in the land of the Harnii.
- Their fat store seems to keep them from ill health and disease. Their hearts are up to the challenge of supplying a large harn.
- They have disease, old age, and death, much as we do.
- They form bonds in pairs and then raise families. Their social structure is much like what we've come to consider an oddity: the nuclear family. And they pair-bond for what appears to be mutual concern and enjoyment...if not to say love...and the little Harnii are the object of much devotion and pleasure.
- There are malefactors. They are frequently incarcerated when apprehended. But the harshest punishment they issue is having a harn surgically removed; it then never regrows normally, but like a plant on earth will send forth three or four shoots, like the horns on a Jacob sheep.
...Certainly, a stigma for life, unless one might have some further surgical procedure.
- The Harnii have a spiritual life, a complete mystery to me. But they do worship in congregations and pray to what I do not know. They have no images, graven or otherwise.
- Their food is delicious, far better than anything I've ever tasted on Earth. So far, I've felt no ill effects.
- The Harnii—even the most disinterested scientists in the medical community—are fascinated with my presence and condition. Yet not once has one of them as much as suggested that I must stay when I begin to fade. However, they do seem sad to see me go.

- They know the value of work and how important it is for each individual to make the best contribution he or she is able.

I am sure I'll discover more as time goes on. So far these are a people who have made efforts to be sure I'm comfortable. they even have a capacious robe made from my visitations. And while they look at me when I walk among them, it's with curiosity and not horror or revulsion. Little children like to come up and pat me. They don't pinch or poke, just pat.

All of which leads me to this modest proposal: I intend to stay with them. Clear has given her encouragement. The medical school team is thrilled by the prospect.

Today. Later on, this afternoon, I will travel to the Harnii. I will not freely come back.

There are, of course, several contingencies. What happens, for example, if I am really travelling out of my body and my body here withers and dies. Will I die there, too? Or, say, I discover that the Harnii are really cannibals and the reason they're glad to see me is because I represent a large meal? Will I be able to leave in a hurry and come back to Earth after such a time as a week, a month, a year? What will happen if I cannot?

The worst things I can imagine about all this are dying and death. Heaven knows I can encounter those here quickly enough. And even if the transition represents sure death, I may well choose it. As it is, even Dr. Lassiter gives me a limited span before my body betrays me. Already there are ominous warnings...varicose veins, swelling of my feet and ankles, a certain distant hollow thumping of my heart in the middle of the night.

I have no fear of a fatal betrayal. My body has done me dirt all my life. Even if Clear should prove false, I have had the chance to love. If I die a fool, I am content.

And, lastly, before I go, I must make provisions for my worldly goods. Since it may be some time till I'm either found (if my body stays here) or missed (if my body goes), I've left the house in a reasonable order...nothing in the refrigerator to spoil. I will depart from my lawn chair, as has been my habit. If I am gone or dead, I leave the bulk of my worldly possessions to my only living relative, my cousin Myrna of Minneapolis. She is to dispose of all as she sees fit. The house has already been put in her name as has the car. Neither one is completely paid for, but she's free to sell them and take the equity. I ask only that she burn my clothes, not send them to a thrift shop. I know I could ask her to give them away to help another fat man, but those clothes have been such an object of shame that I want them destroyed. They deserve it.

And, just one more thing: if you find this could you forward it to Dr. Edwin Lassiter at the Medical Arts Building on Fairbanks? I would appreciate it.

And this note to Dr. Lassiter: Thank you for all the help you have offered and tried to offer. Our regular conversations left me better off. You took a real—not simply clinical—interest in me. I was able to stand it just a little longer because of you. I leave to you my pencil sketches of the Harnii. They are in my bedroom in a folio on my dresser.

I believe I am going to a far, far better place. But from there I don't know. At the end of my life things may get sticky about just where my soul is to go.

Thank you.

Hugo.

*Stanley, the message ends there. As Hugo's medical advisor I'm relieved that we did not discover a body. The police have undertaken the job of finding a very large missing person, probably naked, not the sort who could be easily hidden. And as I implied before, Hugo's obesity is not the sort that will allow him to melt away to nothing, and then to easily assume a new persona. It's my opinion that he has either very cleverly done away with himself (which doesn't seem likely) or he's gone where he said he was going, as improbable as that seems.*

*Of course, I wish he had come and talked with me, although I recognize one of my limitations in general conversation is that I shy away from the personal. And this would have been deeply personal. He probably sensed that this would have been far out of my professional ambit. I'd like to think that I might have offered some informed counsel, whatever that might have been. Or perhaps there really wasn't time for a consultation after he'd made up his mind, and he took the tide at the changing.*

*I did enter his bedroom and found the folio. The images, rendered in blind contour, are astounding. And all that from memory, for he evidently could not take or bring anything with him as he traveled. The Harnii are uniformly thin, striking in their angularity. On the top of the neat stack was an arresting image of a lovely young...woman. I send on a copy. She is identified as Clear.*

*In perplexity, I remain,*

*Edwin Lassiter, M.D.*

Clear

# The Professor's Dog

## A Story in Three Parts

### Part 1: Ella

Fatum.

I know my fate. Death will come soon: a last seizure. I know they are increasing in frequency, and the doctors have said that they are increasing in severity as a result of a growing tumor, an inoperable growing tumor. They have tested, scanned, measured, compared, monitored throughout an episode. And their verdict is unflinching: death.

And with it will end the knowledge of all I hold dear: my work, my students and colleagues, even my old loves.

Of my work it seems there is no end of discovery, even though my field is history. In particular, I study the interactions between the French trappers and the Native Americans, the Anishinabek, in the *pays d'en haut,* or the upper country of the Great Lakes basin and up into Canada. I have researched all manner of contemporary documentation from anecdotal accounts—letters, diary entries, long-repeated family stories—to treaties and other official reports. I have written books and journal articles, made presentations, and taught. And this is what I have learned. The ways those Native Americans balanced the interests of the French against the English and even the Spanish for almost 200 years revealed a

# The Professor's Dog

# A Story in Three Parts

## Part 1: Ella

Fatum.

I know my fate. Death will come soon: a last seizure. I know they are increasing in frequency, and the doctors have said that they are increasing in severity as a result of a growing tumor, an inoperable growing tumor. They have tested, scanned, measured, compared, monitored throughout an episode. And their verdict is unflinching: death.

And with it will end the knowledge of all I hold dear: my work, my students and colleagues, even my old loves.

Of my work it seems there is no end of discovery, even though my field is history. In particular, I study the interactions between the French trappers and the Native Americans, the Anishinabek, in the *pays d'en haut,* or the upper country of the Great Lakes basin and up into Canada. I have researched all manner of contemporary documentation from anecdotal accounts—letters, diary entries, long-repeated family stories—to treaties and other official reports. I have written books and journal articles, made presentations, and taught. And this is what I have learned. The ways those Native Americans balanced the interests of the French against the English and even the Spanish for almost 200 years revealed a great mastery of diplomacy. Whatever happened afterward, after the treaties—the Chicago Treaty of 1833 and the Detroit Treaty of 1855—that dispossessed the Anishinaabe of their lands, that was a different matter altogether.

I have had generations of students to fill classes I've taught about my area of research and other topics in American history. I have been particularly heartened at the handfuls of students who would sign up for whatever courses I taught. I heard one young man tell another that he was majoring in Ella Maxwell. That's me. I seemed to have many of the best students, and they responded to the challenges I put before them. They even have made groundbreaking discoveries on their own. Every time one of my undergraduate students has a refereed paper accepted, we cheer. All of us.

That includes my colleagues who give the meaning to collegial. They are supportive, cheerful, not consumed with proprietary claims and territoriality. There is very little meanness in the whole department of the eight of us. They are fine scholars, too, most of whom have endearing eccentricities. They have been most helpful in these recent days, picking up whatever I leave as slack. On days of a seizure, or the next, when I am pretty well wiped out, they will take a class or excuse me from a departmental meeting. They understand that things are not good and getting worse, but I haven't told them of my expiration date rapidly approaching. At some level, though, they KNOW.

Of my old loves, what is there to say? A former husband, remarried now and with children, but who is still a friend? How he pulled that off, I do not know. Well, I do, and I don't; it has to do with his now-wife. She, too, has become a friend. She understands that I am no threat. And after a seizure, I am as likely to call her as anyone else, such as a recently assigned home-health aide. There have been others who were and are close, a few good friends who have stood by me.

And then there is Honey, the most serviceable of friends just now. A serviceable service dog, a seizure dog. She can tell when my brain is about to light up, and she alerts me that I need to find a soft spot to land.

She is a real beauty, a Labrador retriever and almost a perfect representation of the breed. Her color is yellow to red, kind of like tupelo honey. She is a big dog, but not fat; I have been assiduous about her diet.

Her only defect, if you could call it that, is a quarter-sized patch of hair on her forehead that seems to go a different direction and reveals itself in the right light roughly like a miniature map of Wisconsin. It adds individuality but would keep her off the winner's stand in a show.

She has been with me for three years now. She has gone with me everyplace I needed to go: walking to the office, to coffee shops, into the classrooms, at meetings and events, even dinners (with her nose twitching).

And while she exhibits plenty of individuality, she is one of a type. I understand from my biologist colleagues that Lab brains exhibit emotions that are close to those of humans. I believe she understands my moods, and I hers. Honey and I can spend long moments staring into each other's eyes.

She does her work with me, but she doesn't give an indication that it's all she lives for. In that way she is unlike some other service dogs I've encountered. In less serious things she is stubborn, sometimes even bull-headed. But she is a friend. I sometimes call her Sister Dog. She never has failed me. Sometimes, though, after a seizure, I wonder what's been going on behind those gold-brown eyes. Does what she sees concern her? I believe it does.

And I wonder most of all if I am alone with her when I have my last seizure how it will affect her; will she be able to handle it? I fear my dying might do her great harm. Beyond that, I hate to leave, and I hate to leave her.

## Part 2: Honey

Ella died on a spring night. She had just let me in from being outside in the backyard. We were getting ready for bed. I sensed a seizure—the third that week—and warned her, bringing the portable phone from the low table. She thought there would be time to get into bed, and there almost was. The seizure dropped her at the edge of her bed, and she hit her head against the steel bedframe as she went down. Worse, though, the alert device she wore about her neck was trapped between the box spring and the frame. It wouldn't release, and I couldn't trigger it. I pawed at it, tugged the lanyard with my teeth, but there was no getting to the button. She also had fallen on the phone and when I nosed it out from beneath her, the phone wouldn't dial. It had been damaged or the battery was dislocated. I couldn't summon help, other than by barking. First, I ran to the front door and barked. And then the back. One of the neighbors should have heard. Between barks I paused to listen, but nobody was home in the apartments on either side.

I ran back to Ella. This was the worst ever. She was on her back, thrashing. I lay down prone on top of her with my head to hers, my paws over her shoulders. The last of the seizure, the most powerful pulse, caused her to flail toward me and knocked her head into mine. In that instant, it seemed all of her pain was seared into my brain. The jolt rendered both of us unconscious. I have to believe she slid rapidly into death; I only slowly recovered from blackness to a daze, and then a realization that Ella was no more.

I didn't know it then, but my howls had run on for nearly an hour when Jim, one of our neighbors, returned. He carried the key to our apartment with him, and even before he unlocked his own door, he let himself in ours and found us. He dragged me away from Ella and set about doing CPR. But it was too late. Much too late.

Even if he had been there when she seized, there was likely nothing he could have done. It was her end.

I stayed where he dragged me, still crying aloud—a howl to a human. I didn't even know that he'd moved me. And I was still in a daze when someone—I have no idea who—came to take me away. It was a few days before I began to track again, and then I found myself in an animal shelter. I was in a pen far to the back. I know now that's a bad place to be: it's where they keep animals who cannot be controlled. Dogs often are there for observation—away from the general public—and are first for execution, even immediate execution if things do not go well.

I remember thirst. I had been lying on my side and I remember opening an eye and seeing a water bowl. That's what I wanted. Water. To get it I'd have to get up and walk. When I was standing, I realized that I suddenly knew that the water was in what was called a bowl. Other words flooded in...cage, animal shelter, execution, euthanasia, color, paint, dog run, clock, blanket...concept after concept. I staggered to the bowl and lapped the cool. New words...swallow, dehydration. I had never learned anything so fast. But I didn't learn it; I already knew it. As I continued drinking, I listened to the other dogs, many of them whining, trying to find out where they were, why they were there. All were uneasy. The smell of death was heavy. This was before many of the shelters—including this one—went "no kill." Many dogs had come to their ends here.

My thirst slaked, I remembered that Ella had died. With great sorrow I lay down and rested my head on my paws. My head still hurt from whatever happened.

I had taken water, but I didn't take food, not for the next three or four days. I wasn't hungry. Finally, one of the caretakers, a volunteer who reminded me somewhat of Ella—something in the way she moved, fed me from her hand. It would have been rude to turn away. And before the week was out, I was eating regularly, but not much.

During those few days, things kept coming to me. I had so much knowledge, about as much as a human, I guessed. I thought I knew pretty much everything that Ella had in her head.

Before my own singularity—the two into one—life was much simpler. I was a dog, I knew I was a dog, all I wanted to be was a dog. I was a service dog, meticulously trained as a seizure dog. I was assigned to Ella. And we had fun and played a lot when I wasn't called on to work. But I was ever ready.

Most of the time I could warn her of the probability of a seizure. I could smell it as the acid/electric scent rolled off her body.

...Not that I knew what those words meant then or that Ella was Professor Ella Maxwell, a history professor at the university. Or that our walks were to her office, to her classes, and meetings...or to the doctor or hospital. In fact, there was hardly anything I could put into the words of a dog's vocabulary of several hundred words. All I knew was this: she was my human, and I went with her to help her and love her. And she helped me and loved me, too. She was so good to me; I glowed in her attention. She was everything to me. And I was her Honey.

And I knew the smell of trouble. Now I know that she suffered from a seizure disorder, the result of a tumor. It was at the moment of her final *grand mal* seizure when the pulse of energy that usually jolted from one side of her brain, across the corpus callosum to the other hemisphere, somehow—probably because of the tumor—was routed to the outside of her brain, through the tissues and skull. And then, in some strange completion of the circuit, the energy entered my head, which had been pressed against hers. The result of this discharge was a migration of a full personality from one living entity to another, from one species to another. Had anything like this happened before? It seemed impossible.

But I was living proof. And consider: a dog's brain is not radically different from a human's. There are analogous structures for the content to migrate to. Yes, the dog brain is smaller, but size does not always determine capacity. If there was extra content, I realized that I simply wouldn't know what I was missing that had been Ella. What there was, was plenty. And what I didn't immediately recall, I could access; there was always more at the edges of what I knew, and, with concentration, I could bring it into view. It felt as if I could access all that had been Ella.

She was not always dominant. In almost all things the higher intelligence would rule over the lesser. But, for all things olfactory, the dog of me reigned supreme. I could access memories of smells from Ella's childhood, scents she held dear, and they were but a pale whiff of what I could smell every day. A dog's nose is what? A hundred-thousand times more sensitive? That part of our brain is 40 times the size of humans'. And our forward-thrust noses and jaws contain a whole laboratory for smell diagnostics…the sensor is a pre-brain of a sort. And each of our nostrils operates independently. We can locate the scent by determining at which nostril it arrived first. That's why dogs move our heads back-and-forth when we're determining the source of a smell.

But I realized that visually, humans had it all over us when it came to color.

But what good would this knowledge be if I were selected for elimination at the shelter? I knew quickly after I started eating again that I needed to find a way out, and not only a way, but the best way. For all the words I knew, I had such limited speech. My first efforts were met by my keepers with sidelong looks and indrawn breath. Then I'd vocalize in what sounded like a grumble, not a bark or a growl, but a kind of complaint. I made them uneasy. That wouldn't serve my interests.

And I was well and truly stuck. My paws were not hands; there was no easy way to release the cage latch. And there would be other doors, other locks. So, I watched, waited, wagged my tail, laid my ears back in submission, allowed myself to enjoy tummy rubs (always and forever a favorite; Ella was the gentlest of stomach strokers). I would show myself unafraid, domesticated, civil (if only they knew by how much), and willing.

In a matter of a few days, I was moved to a front-room pen to be considered for adoption. I had no fear that I'd be picked, but by whom?

One of the first days in the pet population I recognized a visitor, a worker with the service dog organization. He was telling the director as they walked in my direction. "It was really good that you could take her. We'd have done it, but we didn't learn that Ella had died for almost a week. And now there doesn't seem to be any need to disrupt her again. I suppose we could take her for retraining but at five she's an old dog. And I never thought she was THAT good a service dog. So, I'm not sure we could even place her again. I always thought she just wanted to be a family pet."

"Should we let people know about her history?" asked the director.

"I don't see why not," said the service-dog man. "You don't have to go into details, but families are always interested when they're getting a dog that's been well trained, even if she's independently minded. Now, if you don't find a new owner for her, we'll take her back and find one. But I'm pretty sure you won't have any problems. Just look at her."

I wagged and barked in agreement.

So, I wasn't likely to be put down. And I was unlikely to be put back in training or service. My visitor was right; I didn't really want to be a service dog. Working for Ella was pretty much at the outside limit of what I wanted to do. I didn't have to help her out of bed more than a couple times after seizures. She dressed herself and mostly took care of her own needs. I had always been independent minded. Sometimes I got called "a real stinker" when I did what I wanted instead of what Ella wanted. For instance, I did have a little trick I liked to play. If I wanted her to get up and feed me, and she was lazing in bed, I'd get my nose under the edge of the covers just under her chin and then use my snout to flip them, peel them back, all the way to the bottom of the bed. Oh, she could curse, but she would laugh every time. And I'd get fed.

She would call me a Labra-pig retriever. Can you imagine? Most of us aren't very good at self-monitoring when it comes to food. But we are better than good when it comes to begging. So, we manipulate our owners. But it's a mixed manipulation. Sure, we're looking for food, but we love you, too, with all our hearts and souls.

When I looked into Ella's eyes, it was as if she were giving me a hug. I knew Ella loved me so much. She was particularly tuned in, maybe because of her altered brain functioning. I thought I was the luckiest dog in the world

And then that last week.... With the increase in seizures, she had been growing weaker, and it took her far longer to come back. There were the two seizures before the fatal one, and each of them was worse than anything that had come before. The end came so quickly. I was distraught.

Even though in her last seizure, I had gained the additional mind of a human, it was no exchange I wanted. But it was made; she had been transferred to me. But it was not just Ella's knowledge and memories that I carried. Somehow—not in a hostile or overt way—she was still there, still conscious and aware. She did not interfere; if anything, she clarified my thoughts. She was not unwelcome. So, we reasoned together. Or, sometimes she reasoned, and I observed.

Now, we reasoned that I would have to convince someone or a family that I was a good dog. And it would have to be the right prospective owner. There was no escaping that I was to become someone's property.

To get what I/we wanted I needed to give people what they wanted when they walked through the shelter looking for a dog. As a yellow Lab, I was often the focus of attention. Because people were drawn to me, I had to choose carefully. There might be only one opportunity for a way out.

At first it baffled the shelter director when I would—seemingly without cause—get up from my seated position at the door and walk to the back of the cage and hang my head. It was all I could do to indicate my non-choice of a potential owner. Usually, before they could see me, I had decided about them, and behaved accordingly. Some came in reeking of alcohol, maybe not noticeable to other humans, but it oozed out of their pores. Others sent out massive indifference cloaked in enthusiasm, as if someone thought they should have a dog, so they were coming to get a dog. One woman—and I felt truly bad about this—had a cancer she probably didn't know about. But I could smell it.

Another man came with the smell of so many other dogs on him that I concluded he was buying for a medical company. I knew from the fear scents on him that other dogs had suffered pain. Many dogs, much pain. And I pitied his selections. He wanted me, but I wouldn't budge from the rear of the cage.

The shelter director was getting the idea that I was making a choice as much as the people at the front of the cage. "No," he said to me, having no idea that I could fully understand him, "I won't force you from the cage to be carted off." I was grateful and showed him with wags and cheerful yips when those I didn't choose had left.

There were others who had many cats at home, or several other dogs. I thought I could stand one cat, but no other dogs. And many didn't have young children. But children were now a "must."

I had begun to form a plan and a purpose for what remained of my life. That involved children. I hadn't lived with them. But I understood that Ella had always wanted—more than anything else—to be a mother. But there had been no children. I felt her longing. More than anything I, too, wanted to be with them.

They had to be children who were being raised with care; there is nothing worse for a dog than a cruel child unless it's a cruel adult.

So, when Annabelle toddled down the line of cages, her pregnant mother, Kendra, in hot pursuit, I knew. Dogs can smell love. I made sure I was "sitting pretty," at least for the first few minutes. Then I couldn't hold it in. I didn't even try to control my tail as it swished across the floor of the kennel. I squirmed and smiled. I happy-barked and then I put my paw on the door. I wanted so much to come out and just be with them. Annabelle's mother carefully pulled her back from the edge of my cage while a volunteer told her of part of my history.

I regained my sit, cocked my head to listen and only after she was finished, did I stand at the front of the cage, my tail again flailing. I poked my nose through at toddler height, sniffed a couple times and stuck out my tongue to caress Annabelle's proffered hand. She giggled and laughed.

"My dog!" she said. I pulled my nose back through the wire, sat and squirmed, wagging happily. I nodded and sneezed in agreement.

"Hello, Honey," said her mother, bending over to get closer to me, noting my name on the cage door. I sat, my tail still wagging. I had to ask myself: what kind of young mother, again pregnant, would be willing to take on the extra care of a dog? Kendra would. She was care itself.

But that didn't mean things would happen immediately. There was her husband, Jeff, to be consulted. I learned later he had known his wife and daughter were headed for the shelter and, in theory, approved of the concept. The reality would require him to come for a visit, too.

I waited impatiently.

It took a few days before this little family returned. I behaved in all the right ways, and even if Jeff wasn't taken with me, he was taken with his daughter's delight and his wife's quiet assurance. So, at last, out I went with what I thought was pretty much a perfect family for a newly minted family dog. Because of my age, the family got me at a senior discount.

Oh, I had made the right choice, but I could not at that time predict that not only would there be one more child, there would be four more, for a total of five...all daughters, all raised with gentle care, discipline, and encouragement. I was in the middle of all of that.

The first few months we spent getting to know each other. At first, I was relegated to the basement for nights. I was to stay off all furniture. But those rules became more relaxed with the arrival of each "next" child. I watched for each birth and the next pregnancy. Heck, I knew before Kendra did that another child was on the way.

Kendra and Jeff had to be very strict about the girls not feeding me because I easily would start to gain weight. They all knew that extra weight on a Lab is the cause of so many ailments: osteoarthritis, cancers, diabetes, heart disease, hypertension. Even knowing that wouldn't stop me from begging; I was powerless in the face of food.

The only thing I loved more than food was the girls. When Kendra put them down for naps, I would sneak up on their beds, one at a time, and snuggle as close to them as possible. I would put my head against theirs, thinking that just perhaps something of Professor Ella would move into them. And it seemed to work. The girls were very smart, and they knew many things—good things—beyond their years. They loved stories, the heart of all history. So, maybe....

The girls never needed a lead on my collar when I was with them, but often affected one for the notice to those outside the family that THIS dog was under control. A few years ago, I was off leash, and the older girls and I were playing down the block—not immediately in front of the house. A man approached. I sensed something in him that was violent and eager to hurt. I put myself in front of my charges, hair bristling, and steadily growling. Then I ran at him. He bolted. I chased him half a block before I returned. My actions were big conversation around the dining table that night. That time Jeff DID feed me from the table. He said I was a hero. And by that time, I was allowed to sleep upstairs at night with the girls. I took turns, seeing who needed what. I would spend a little time with my head pressed to theirs. The Professor still was inclined to teach.

One night two years ago, the youngest, Eleanor—Nellie to you and me—was ill with a fever. That's when Jeff learned more of the scope of my role. I knew Nellie was sick, and she was sicker than her parents knew. They gave her a last dose of fever reducer for the night, tucked her into her crib, and gave her a kiss on her fevered forehead. Jeff was going to close the door and wanted me out of the room before he did so. He called me, but I refused to move. He came toward me and bent over to grab my collar. I didn't growl; I never do that unless in play, but I refused to move, and I whined so loudly that Jeff let go. I looked steadily at him to tell him that I had to be there. Had. To. Be.

"All right, you silly dog. You stay and I'll leave the door open."

The house was still when Nellie's fever suddenly rose. I knew from the smell that a seizure was imminent. At the first twitch, I set up a howl and ran for Kendra and Jeff's bedroom. Their door was ajar, and I pushed it open, barking. Jeff was galvanized out of bed and down the hall, me leading the way. I could tell Nellie's spell was nowhere near the kinds of attacks that felled Ella. This was a fever seizure. Her seizing stopped as soon as her father picked her up. Then, holding her, Jeff walked to the bathroom for a wet cold compress. I accompanied him and when he returned to her bedroom I sat by the crib. Gently, he cooled her. Kendra took over in a few minutes while he made a phone call to the emergency medical line. Yes, they should bring her in.

Before they left, Jeff called a neighbor to come in, but it would be a few minutes. He turned to me and said, "Tom is coming over, so let him in, but guard the house."

I woofed. I was worried for Nellie, but I knew that she would be in good hands. I felt a wash of relief. And I welcomed Tom in when he arrived.

There were no lasting effects from the seizure, but from that day forward, Jeff began talking to me as if I understood and was a part of his team. I often answered him with a mumble, a soft bark, a sidewise twist and nod of the head. With regularity he told Kendra, "I'm sure Honey understands every word I say to her." Kendra had spent enough time with me to know it was likely. In the neighborhood, I was something of a sensation, but I'd never gratify with a performance of my comprehension to the world at large.

And through the years I have endured what might be considered great indignities that family dogs suffer: dress-up tea parties, having my nails painted, being left at a boarding kennel when the family went away (although less and less of that in these latter years because if I couldn't accompany them, the girls did not want to go). But on the other side I had the treasure of a full heart and great happiness. I was loved extravagantly. I was joyously, exultantly complete. I was where I wanted to be.

And I was a family dog, a good family dog, and I knew it. Who's a good girl? I was.

As a family dog with a little extra, I was able to give a last gift to those I love.

The day was just beautiful, once again early summer or late spring. Warm. All the scents in the air, birds carrying on. The five girls were out without jackets or sweaters; it was that warm. They were playing with friends across the street. I was to the house-side of the sidewalk, keeping a remote eye on things. As an older dog, I didn't get involved any longer with their running games, but I loved to watch them race about.

I caught some movement from the corner of my eye...there was Nellie, now almost three. She had left her sisters and was standing by the curb with the evident intention of crossing the street to come home. Her sisters were not watching her. She was standing by the bumper of a car parked across the street in front of our house. From behind the parked car I saw another turn at the corner and accelerate towards us. Nellie was hidden from the view of the driver. Moving car and child were destined to intersect if she moved into the street.

She did.

I looked on with panic building. Was there any way? Maybe yes. But ONLY if....

I launched toward Nellie and a split second before the car would have hit her, I butted her back and out of the way.

I didn't clear the car, though. My hips were smashed against the bumper. The left front tire rolled over my legs. The pain was blinding. I tried to stand, but there was nothing to stand with or on. I felt pieces of bone grinding together in the effort.

Nellie set up a wail, and I tried to drag myself with my front legs toward the sound of her voice. I couldn't move far. As some of the pain turned to shock, I was able to see again. Kendra had been standing by the door to the house and only momentarily had been distracted. She raced first to Nellie, who was startled but all right, and then to me.

The driver had stood on her brakes. When she stopped and jumped out of the car she ran to where I was lying. She was sobbing.

"I almost killed her. I almost killed her."

I didn't know if she was talking about Nellie or about me.

Kendra called Jeff, and within a few minutes, he was there from work. I lay on my side and the pain was coming in waves so strong that I couldn't keep my eyes open for long. I think they rolled up into my head. When I would regain focus, I could see the girls had all gathered around me.

The driver of the car stayed right there, trembling. She hadn't been speeding and there was no way for her to have known that Nellie was about to enter her path. She told the story again and again of seeing the child and the streaking dog.

I let out a groan when Jeff put his arms beneath me. I know he was trying to be gentle, but the shifting sent me to the edge of consciousness. I know he put me on a blanket on the backseat of his car. And with Kendra calling ahead we went to Dr. Cotter's, a place I knew well and didn't fear. I tried to wag my tail, but I don't think it moved. My back legs were growing numb, not a good sign, except that it dimmed some of the sharp spasms.

After a manual exam that indicated a busted hip and shattered leg bones, there was a shot for pain. Jeff explained what had happened, how I was injured. Dr. Cotter shook her head and called for X-rays to see how badly busted I was. I did not squirm during the procedure. And afterward, Jeff put his head to mine, telling me how good I was and how much he loved me. He was sad and worried. I wanted to tell him something, anything.

The vet came in to confer. She brought the X-rays and put them up on the light panel. "Honey's whole back end is in little pieces," she said. "Even if we operate to put them back together, there is no guarantee that she could walk. Here's where the spine has been damaged, too. That means that she will not be able to go outside and take care of business. And that means that she's going to be both messy and prone to infections. ...To say nothing of the pain. She is in intense pain now, agony. And that may not get better for a long time, if ever."

Jeff looked at her questioningly.

"If she were my dog, I would choose to relieve the pain," she said.

Jeff nodded. "Let me call Kendra. She needs to agree, and I think she should be here. What about the girls? Should they be here, too?"

"It all depends. We'll sedate her heavily so that she'll be in a deep sleep and then we'll give her an injection to stop her heart. Sometimes, with old dogs like Honey, there is some twitching, or an intake of breath, or even a little seizure, but that's rare. And even then, they just relax and are gone."

The pain wasn't quite so intense by the time Kendra and the girls arrived. Jeff explained to them that I was hurt very badly and wasn't able to get better. The best thing they could do was to gently put me to sleep. And that I wouldn't wake up. I was going to die. "But all living things die," he said. "This is just Honey's time."

But I wanted to do more with my girls, teach them more. I only have done some of what I intended.

Everyone was crying, Nellie most of all. She knew what had happened in a three-year-old way. She begged her father to hold her. He bent over and picked her up. She turned to watch as the first needle slid in. I watched the tears in her eyes.

Hard to contemplate my now-understanding of time with my dog-sense of my life. The human part says I'm at the end. The dog-knowing says all is in order; dogs don't worry about death until it overtakes them, and even then, they don't worry. They simply die, painfully or easily.

## Part 3: Jeff

Nellie was crying, and when Dr. Cotter gave Honey the second shot, she squirmed to get down to the table with the dog. I didn't have a firm enough grasp and she made it, kicking at me when I tried to regain my hold. I was worried in case in her pain and dying that Honey could snap. But I didn't have to worry. Honey took a large final breath, arched her back and extended her paws, shivered…and then let out the air. She was still. Nellie had been hugging Honey tightly, her forehead against the dog's and only with effort could I get her to let go of the dog's neck. She came away dazed.

The other girls surrounded the table. All of us were crying, including Dr. Cotter.

This dog had given her life for my daughter's so willingly. That's the only way I could describe it; she gave no thought for her own life when Nellie's was in the balance. This dog had been with us for eight years, sharing almost every experience of our family. She had made everything better. She was smart, almost eerily so; she was funny, she was fun, and she was protective. I could always count on her to do the right thing…no matter what it was. There never could be another dog like her.

Kendra took Nellie and the rest of the girls to the minivan for the drive home. I was going to bring home Honey's body and bury her at the far end of the garden, a place she liked to lie out in the sun. She was dead weight, there was no rigor yet, and she slid around in my arms. Dr. Cotter finally had to help me; we carried her out on a rug held between us to get her to the car. She rode on the front seat, the same place she'd stand with her head out the window. And even with the window down, I could smell the drugs seeping out of her lungs as her body jostled on the seat. I couldn't let the girls hug her now.

Digging the hole large enough and deep enough was a challenge. I found every tree root in the yard, which meant I had to do a lot of trimming with the saw, bent over in this pit. Toward the end, I was waist deep in the hole, hauling up the sand to the edge of the hole. I had placed Honey's body in a wheelbarrow, and first I had to slide her out on the edge of the hole. Then with everybody watching, I slid her into the grave, moved her to her side. Last thing, I unsnapped her collar, something I probably should have done first. I handed it up to Kendra.

The girls had decided that there needed to be prayers. I couldn't disagree, so we all said some. We prayed for Honey…fields of rabbits to chase, other dogs, little boy and girl angels to play with, soft beds, good food and water, a ball to chase, a wonderful forever. Kendra said that if dogs didn't go to heaven, she wanted to go where they went. And we all cried again when I began the process of filling in the grave. It's so hard to realize that never again would there be that cold nose under the table, or those legs launching her up on the couch, tail wagging with embarrassment that she knew she shouldn't be there but was just going to stay for a little while. There would be no more happy bark when I came home from work.

I sprinkled grass seed over the mounded grave, and we all walked into the house. I needed a shower.

The next few weeks were full of reminders of the precious dog everywhere we turned. …Her bowls, her balls, her tug toys. Kendra forgot sometimes and prepared her food. Once she even called for Honey to come in for dinner before she remembered.

Nellie was most affected by the experience. She seemed confused for a time by everything that had happened, complained of headaches. And there were other changes.

One night I was getting ready to read to the girls. It was Nellie's turn to pick what she'd like to hear.

"So, Nellie, what will it be tonight?" I asked.

She looked at me calmly, and before making her request, she said "I'm not Nellie. I'm Ella."

I wondered where she had heard that nickname and why she chose it now. No one in the family had ever shortened Eleanor to Ella.

And there have been other changes. Even though she's always been bright, she now has taken to standing and looking intently at anything that catches her interest. She wants to know everything about everything. At three and a half, she is teaching herself to read. And she is making great strides, reading more than her next oldest sister, Becca, who is no slouch. Often, when she thinks no one is watching, she appears thoughtful, far away. She tries to catch every breeze, turning into it, as if it contains a secret just for her.

She is the biggest advocate for us getting another dog. It can't be just any dog, she says. She'll know the right one. So, she and Kendra have started making weekly trips to the shelter. She hasn't found the right dog yet, she says, but she will.

As with all the girls, she is a wonder and a delight, but she is the most different of us. I wonder what she'll become, or what will become of her. Two very different questions.

But I don't worry. I feel like she is being watched over, protected. Or maybe I'm just being hopeful.

Made in the USA
Middletown, DE
02 February 2024

48429112R00092